UNSPARKED

11

WEIGH THE ODDS

CORINNA TURNER

unSeen

PRAISE FOR CORINNA TURNER'S BOOKS

LIBERATION: nominated for the *Carnegie Medal Award 2016*
ELFLING: 1st prize, Teen Fiction, *CPA Book Awards 2019*
I AM MARGARET & *BANE'S EYES:* finalists, *CALA Award 2016/2018*
LIBERATION & *THE SIEGE OF REGINALD HILL*: 3rd place, *CPA Book Awards 2016/2019*

Corinna Turner was awarded the **St. Katherine Drexel Award** in **2022.**

PRAISE FOR *ELFLING*

I was instantly drawn in

EOIN COLFER, author of *Artemis Fowl* and former Children's Laureate of Ireland

PRAISE FOR *WEIGH THE ODDS*

Josh, Darryl and Harry have been in some pretty tough situations before. But I think this is the hardest thing they've had to face yet! I was on the edge of my seat the whole time.

MARIE C. KEISER, author of the Heaven's Hunter series

I only meant to start this and now it's past midnight and I'm wishing for book 12! Excellent adventure story!

KARINA FABIAN, author of the Vern stories and other books

This instalment grabs the reader by the throat with edge-of-the-seat, heart-pounding suspense on every page. How can Josh, Darryl, and Harry survive this time when the odds are stacked so high against them? I HIGHLY recommend this series!

KATY HUTH JONES, author of *Treachery and Truth*

Corinna Turner packs her classic punch with heart-in-your-throat suspense and fierce action. This sci-fi survival thriller will grip you to the last page.

GABRIELLA BATEL, award-winning author of the Don't series

ALSO BY CORINNA TURNER:

I AM MARGARET series
For older teens and up

Brothers *(A Prequel Novella)**
1: I Am Margaret*
2: The Three Most Wanted*
3: Liberation*
4: Bane's Eyes*
5: Margo's Diary*
6: The Siege of Reginald Hill*
7: A Saint in the Family*
'The Underappreciated Virtues of Rusty Old Bicycles' *(Prequel short story) Also found in the anthology:* Secrets: Visible & Invisible*

I Am Margaret: The Play *(Adapted by Fiorella de Maria)*

UNSPARKED series
For tweens and up

Main Series:
1: Please Don't Feed the Dinosaurs*
2: A Truly Raptor-ous Welcome*
3: PANIC!*
4: Farmgirls Die in Cages*
5: Wild Life*
6: A Right Rex Rodeo*
7: FEAR
8: A Different Kind of Camouflage
9: A Different Kind of Freedom
10: What's Done is Done
11: Weigh the Odds
12: A Nest of Piranha'saurs†

Prequels:
BREACH!*
A Mom With Blue Feathers
A Very Jurassic Christmas*

Short Stories (ebook only):
'Liam and the Hunters of Lee'Vi'
'A Truly Clawful Christmas'*
'A Very Jurassic Lent'
Also available as a paperback:
Three Clawsome Tales*

FRIENDS IN HIGH PLACES series
For tweens and up

1: The Boy Who Knew (Carlo Acutis)*
2: Old Men Don't Walk to Egypt (Saint Joseph)*
3: Child, Unwanted (Margaret of Castello)*
4: A Lion for a Tomb (Ignatius of Antioch)

Do Carpenter's Dream of Wooden Sheep? *(Spin-off, comes between 1 & 2)*

1: El Chico Que Lo Sabia (Spanish)
1: Il Ragazzo Che Sapeva (Italian)

YESTERDAY & TOMORROW series
For adults and mature teens only
Someday: A Novella*
1: Tomorrow's Dead†

OTHER WORKS

For teens and up
Elfling*

'The Most Expensive Alley Cat in London' (Elfling *prequel short story*)

For tweens and up
Mandy Lamb & The Full Moon*

The Wolf, The Lamb, and The Air Balloon (Mandy Lamb *novella*)

For adults and new adults
Three Last Things *or* The Hounding of Carl Jarrold, Soulless Assassin*
A Changing of the Guard*

The Raven & The Yew†

† **Coming Soon**
* **Awarded the Catholic Writers Guild**
Seal of Approval

CONTENTS

JOSHUA

Seb is *here*. In Exception City.

I stare at the unfamiliar yet familiar Habitat Vehicle as it backs into a position across the 'Vi-park from my own HabVi.

What do I do?

Go over and speak to him, I guess. It's the last thing I wanna do, but it'll look too weird if I don't. He can't guess that I know anything more about him than I found out during the month we spent in prison together.

Or does going over there look like I'm trying too hard? He knows I don't like him, and he sure never pretended to like me, though we kept things civil. Just about.

But I'm his co-owner, now, even though I'm a sleeping partner. Ignoring him seems odd.

Why is he even here? This ain't his usual patch. I can't see no sign of no one else in the cab. Is he alone, or is his assistant in the back for some reason? His new assistant. Since he left Wilhelm in prison serving the time for Seb's own hit and run.

If only that were the worst thing Seb's done.

I glance around the empty 'Vi-park. On second thought, I ain't gonna go out there while we're alone. Another 'Vi or two will be along before dark, almost certain. For now, I'll sit tight. My turret windows are polarized, he won't know I'm sitting up here watching him.

Well, not unless he points a heat scope my way. The windows won't block that a hundred percent. Mebbe I should go downstairs so I can pretend I ain't noticed he's arrived without him catching me. I wanna put a sweater on, anyways. This day ain't getting no warmer—a good excuse to leave my shutters closed. No reason he should recognize my 'Vi, right? He ain't never seen it.

I pass an uncomfortable hour in the living area distractedly checking cupboards and putting everything in order after my forced nine-month absence. Not being able to see Seb's 'Vi makes my back feel like ants are crawling up it.

I clean, too. I don't want no strange moldy smells

drawing nosy predators. I give the head a real good clean too, even picking out and sanitizing the hinges of the fold-down toilet bowl with my deep-cleaning kit.

It's a good feeling when I'm done, like the 'Vi is mine again. Even though it always were.

I'm just checking the console—still no storm warnings, it's just my nerves setting me on edge—when the sound of an engine announces another vehicle pulling into the park.

Finally!

I call up the camera feeds and take a look. Elder Harman's 'Vi is maneuvering into position a little way along from mine. It's only when my guts relax that I realize how tightly they've been knotted up.

Although...

"Harman 'Vi to Wilson 'Vi," comes from the interCar radio. "Joshua, you there?"

There goes any possibility of lying low in here and hoping Seb goes away without realizing this is my 'Vi. Reluctantly, I press the talk button, knowing Seb can hear me too. "Hello Harman 'Vi. Joshua here."

"It's good to hear your voice, cub. City-folk finally let you out, did they?"

"Sure did. Thanks be to Saint Des." The city-folk accepted that running away in the 'Vi to work for me were all Darryl and Harry's idea, but because I were eighteen when we lit out, and Darryl and Harry weren't, they still locked me away for nine months when they finally caught up with us. But I don't think they ever really believed that Darryl and Harry's dad had been kidnapped, not just et by a raptor the way Seb made it look.

Elder Harman, his son, and his assistant are soon at my door carrying their folding chairs and fire-making materials, along with a stack of meat packets and other promisingly tasty-looking items.

"C'mon." Elder Harman nods toward the shelter. "Let's get a fire lit and celebrate, cub!"

I don't bother trying to remind an elder that I really am a man now. Twenty's still plenty young, to him.

"Whose is that, by the way?" asks Elder Harman, jerking his head toward Seb's 'Vi. "D'you know 'em?"

"Er, yeah, I guess I do."

"Wanna go invite 'em to join us?"

No.

"Sure." Now that we're gathering under the shelter it really will look bad if I don't speak to Seb. Guess I can't put it off no longer.

Taking a deep breath and squaring my shoulders—*I hope you're got my back, Saint Des*—I walk across the worn pavement toward the 'Vi I technically own twenty-five percent of, even if I ain't allowed to benefit from the share while Seb is alive. I reach up and rap on the side door. Mebbe he's gone off somewhere on foot while I were hiding behind my closed shutters.

No such luck. With a hiss, the door slides back. A

slender man with sun-browned skin leans in the doorway, the familiar thorny rose tattoo winding up the side of his neck. He stares down at me.

"Well, well, cub. Imagine meeting you here. I see they let you out."

He sounds as insincere as usual, and I eye him closely. Did he already know I'd been released the other day?

I try to speak casually.

"Just figured I'd come say hi. We're having some food." I jerk a thumb over my shoulder at the shelter. Mebbe he won't wanna come. "Uh...you know about... about Wilhelm, right?"

Of course he does. He's received the letter about the will, about me being his co-owner now. The prison offered him Wilhelm's remains, too. But since Seb and Wilhelm were co-owners for eight years it seems too weird not to mention it.

Seb's lip curls in that unpleasant way I remember too well. "Sure do." He stares down at me. "I hear you got special permission to be at the hospital with him when he died."

My heart gives a nasty thunk, and I fight harder than ever for calm. The last thing I wanted Seb to know were that Wilhelm mighta had a chance to talk to me at a time when he knew nothing he told me could hurt him no more. But Seb already knows. Some city-guy from the prison he's kept in contact with? Billy and Ku wouldn't be communicating with him, right?

"Yeah, the prison thought someone should be with him." I fight harder than ever to play it cool. "There weren't really nothing I could do, though. But he were able to see the chaplain, get everything straight."

"Made very sure he got everything straight, did you?" Seb's narrow eyes harden.

Aw, *misfire*. Does he think I had something to do with Wilhelm leaving me the share of his 'Vi? Didn't think of that.

"Only with the chaplain. The hospital had sent him a will-writer already. They were very on top of things."

"Bet he wished you'd never turned up when you sicced some priest on him."

I shrug. "He spoke to him for ages and seemed happier after, so I dunno. I were waiting outside." Yeah, hopefully Seb will think Wilhelm spilled his secrets to a priest, not to me. Even Seb understands about the Seal of Confession, right? Or does he?

I clear my throat. I really, really don't wanna say this, but I feel like I have to give Seb one last chance to do the right thing. "The prison warden gave me Wilhelm's urn. Y'know, with his ashes. Do you, uh, wanna take charge of 'em?"

Seb sneers outright, at that. "He was little enough use alive, he's no use at all dead. You may as well just empty it down the head."

I clench my fists, a strange buzzing in my ears,

fighting an almost overwhelming urge to grab Seb by the ankle and yank—then stamp him into the pavement. I force myself to breathe out. And in. And out. Finally, I manage to say,

"I'll take care of it, then."

"Of course you will. Perfect little cub that you are."

I manage something that's more a tight grimace than a smile, and turn away.

"Oh, cub?"

I turn back. "What, old man?" Though Seb ain't much older than Dad woulda been.

He just smirks, of course. "Do you play poker?"

"Only for knick-knacks and pocket change."

Seb smirks even harder. "Yeah? Shame."

I turn and walk away, my back prickling. If he's saying I'm easy to read, then...what did he read, just now, as we talked?

Does he know I know?

Mebbe I shouldn't have gone to speak to him.

Only that woulda kinda told him the same thing, wouldn't it?

+

By the time I get over to the shelter, delicious savory smells already sizzle up from the grill tray over the fire pit. Prime Triceratops burgers, I'd say. My mouth, uncomfortably dry after the conversation with Seb, begins to water.

"Agh, I ain't tasted nothing this good for...for

almost a year," I say, through my first huge mouthful.

Elder Harman claps me on the shoulder. "Eat up, then, cub."

I'm on my third burger when Seb saunters up at last. He accepts a burger from the Harman son wielding the spatula, and deposits his folding chair just on the other side of Elder Harman, who he immediately starts talking with—all charm, of course. Makes me wanna vomit.

I strike up a conversation with the Harman assistant, Melki, who's sitting slightly further away on the other side of the fire, and use that as an excuse to casually move my chair around to join him. Having Seb so close makes me feel like the skin is gonna crawl right off me. At least sitting here with my back to the 'Vi-park means I don't have to look out at that misfiring vehicle that ties the two of us together.

I try to concentrate on what Melki is saying—and on my burger. But it don't taste so good, no more.

What is Seb *doing* here? Since I'm a sleeping partner, I'd assumed he'd just stay in his usual patch and do his thing and pretend I didn't exist, since for all practical intents and purposes I don't. Pretend he were a sole owner, just the way he wants.

Is he gonna offer to buy out my share? Heck, I'd give it to him, just to be free of him, 'cept Wilhelm coulda left it to him, if he'd wanted Seb to have it. And Seb of all men don't deserve to get some'at for nothing.

Melki's waiting for me to reply. What were he talking about? But before I have to respond, footsteps crunch over the pavement behind me and a booming voice calls,

"Josh! We can hardly believe the news! Their dad's alive? After all this time!"

"Darryl and Harry must be on top of the world," adds a softer voice.

I spin around, almost toppling my chair, my heart rate kicking up as several emotions strike me all at once.

Delight—to see my almost-uncles from Technicolor 'Vi, who I ain't seen since the city-folk locked me away.

Dismay—that Seb now knows that Darryl and Harry's neighbor Maurice (who Seb sold their dad to) didn't kill William Franklyn the way he said he were gonna.

Panic—as I try to figure out how to salvage the situation.

I can't help throwing a glance across the fire. Seb's looking at the newcomers with an expression of mild curiosity only—but his shoulders are a little too tense. He heard alright. And understood.

Belatedly, I get up and accept a hug from big, dark-skinned West and equally dark-skinned Trudi, glancing from one to the other.

"I'm so sorry I missed your wedding."

They both smile and wave that away. "We weren't expecting you to pull no jailbreak, Josh."

I go to hug pale-skinned, blond-haired Ed as well, who's ambled up behind, grinning. Gently, since he's probably got some'at small and furry inside his jacket.

"We hoped we'd find you still here," Ed says. "Or we wouldn't have bothered with this quick visit."

"Where's Thiago?" I ask them. "He okay?"

"Sure is," says West. "Just getting on with some jobs at the camp, since we got enough hands in the 'Vi with Trudi along. For now, anyway."

I interpret that easily enough. Trudi's taking advantage of what may be her last few chances to go out hunting for some time, if things happen as they hope in the family line. No doubt they've left Thiago to get their new camp looking as good as possible before I arrive for my first ever peep. Ain't hard for them to guess that they'll be my first stop when I leave Exception City.

"I'm so sorry I couldn't help with setting up your camp, neither," I add, but they grin and wave that away too.

I can't help hugging West and Ed all over again, and they hug me back, hard. "It's real good to see you guys. But you shoulda stayed away. What if the city-folk realize you helped us stay free all that time?" I finish, under my breath.

They shrug. "We weren't here the day you came

outta jail, and by the sounds of things, that social worker won't be in your hair no more, anyways."

"Uh, yeah, how'd you hear about that?" I ask, lowering my voice a little so it's harder for Seb to hear, but not so low it looks weird.

"Met that rural priest friend of yours down at the supply depot. Father—"

"Oh yeah, I see." I cut West off in a real rude way, but at least I stop him naming Father Benedict in front of Seb. I don't even know why I'm quite so worried. I mean, Darryl and Harry's dad being alive...it's gonna be gossip all over the place in no time. Still, no need for Seb to know more about my friends than he has to.

I glance behind them, spotting Technicolor 'Vi parked beside mine. That darn main road. So noisy. From over here in the shelter, you can't even hear a 'Vi pull into that end of the park.

"Friends of yours, Josh?" Seb, speaking with an easy smile, and warm friendly eyes, of course, so I have to introduce everyone. Because I didn't dare keep barely any contact with Technicolor while I were in jail, they greet him with obviously unfeigned ease—so, actually, mebbe it's good they don't know nothing.

I'm looking forward to telling them as soon as we're in private, though. It makes my teeth clench to see them chatting and laughing with that snake.

"Okay, let's have some fun," says Ed, after a while. "Mimicry competition."

"Ah, what's the point?" says Elder Harman's son. "Josh is here."

"So, we're competing for second place, that's all," says Elder Harman, grinning.

My cheeks get hot with embarrassment. "Why don't we do a pair competition?" I suggest quickly. "Two critters, not one."

"You're still gonna win," says Melki dryly. "Ain't no one bad enough to pair with you and lose."

I try very hard not to look at city-born Seb, 'cause mimicry sure ain't something he's ever put much effort into learning. But I catch the flick of his eyes from side to side as he does the numbers. Eight of us. No chance he can sit out. Only one chance he might not be on the losing team, and he's too proud to be beaten even at a friendly little competition like this...

"Wanna pair up, raptor-boy? Us being co-owners and all."

I breathe out carefully—why do I find it so hard to keep my temper around this snake?—and attempt to smile. "Sure."

Disappointment flits across Ed's face—he'd have been my first choice and we sure woulda won together. But he just pairs with Melki instead.

"Dakotaraptor matriarch feeding her chicks," I murmur in Seb's ear, when it's our turn. "You can do a chick, right?"

It's the absolute easiest thing I can think of. Not

that I care if he's humiliated in front of this pack of hunter-borns. But he knows I know what he's capable of, so he'd know I'd set him up to fail.

"Sure." He smirks at me, like he knows perfectly well that he's the last person here I'd have picked for a partner and is enjoying the heck out of my discomfort.

I grit my teeth and shift further away to start the vocalization. All Seb has to do is peep like a very young chick, and Dakota chicks sound a lot like humans at that age. I provide all the more complicated dialogue as the mother returns to her nest, greets the adult pack members, checks on the chicks, feeds them, scolds them a bit...

We win. Of course. Seb basks in the limelight, like everyone here don't know exactly how easy his role were.

"I'll give it to you, cub." Seb toasts me with his mug. "You may be the worst at poker, but you sure could convince anyone alive a raptor was standing behind them."

He sure does think I'm easy to read. I glance at West and the others. Mebbe...mebbe I shouldn't tell them nothing about Seb. Not until he's gone. They might all three have better poker faces than me, but he'll be able to tell if their manner changes toward him.

Yeah, I gotta say nothing. Once he clears off to his usual hunting grounds, hopefully he won't be back.

It gets later and we finally disperse to our 'Vis, me

feigning tiredness to avoid being alone with West and the others, since they mighta picked up on my nerves around Seb. But the question just keeps nipping at me.

Why *is* Seb here?

+

Seb's 'Vi is gone.

That's the first thing I notice in the morning, when I climb up to the turret with a cup of Joe shortly before the late winter dawn.

My insides unknot. He ain't left no chairs out or nothing to mark his spot, the way he would he if were just going for supplies or to the shop. He's gone. Good. Hopefully that's the last I'll ever see of him. Mebbe he were just traveling through on his way to fulfill some contract or other.

Assuming he's still hunting normally. At least some of the time. He crossed a line when he kidnapped Darryl and Harry's father. How long will someone like him resist the lure of easy money?

I shudder and sip my Joe, checking the weather. No, no storm warnings. My body must be really on edge, 'cause I keep expecting something to flash up. Low level warning of a potential killer-chiller up in Tana state, nothing nearer. And the chances are, that will come to nothing, this early in the season. It's not even December yet.

Soon Technicolor are closing their shutters and raising their stabilizers—got a time-limited contract in hand—so I head over to say goodbye. No point mentioning Seb now—not when he's gone. I'll tell them all about it when I visit.

"And when you're convinced that Darryl and Harry can spare you," says West sternly, "you head straight to our camp, you hear? Thiago can come be your assistant for a while, until you find someone who's a good fit. But don't you be driving around alone a moment more than you hafta."

I grimace. "Yeah, yeah. I've got a scar on my foot to remind me of that lesson."

And then they're gone. The Harman 'Vi bids me farewell not long after.

And I'm alone.

Well, not for long. I check the time. I need to head into the city to meet Father Ben at some cafe. Unfortunately, he ain't got time to come out here to me in between a meeting with his bishop and some'at else.

I open the store cupboard and glance into the back. The cheerful gift bag covered in bright, happy-looking 'saurs is present and correct, hiding the ugly plastic gallon jar inside it. "I'm gonna see Father Ben about a burial now, Wilhelm," I tell the urn. "Make this right."

I shake my head as I let myself out of the 'Vi and leap to the ground. I still can't believe the city-folk just burnt Wilhelm to a crisp and stuck him in that thing. It ain't right.

Father Ben said God can deal with it. But I'll still

feel better when Wilhelm's in the ground, where he should be. I tap the door control to lock it, and head across the pavement at a brisk walk. I gotta get a bus, then I can walk the rest of the way.

I make it on time—almost. I always forget how slow it is moving through the city. So many roads to cross. People in the way. But I'm only a couple of minutes late when I enter D'Nuts Coffee. I barely have to scan the tables to spot Father Ben, who's as tall and broad as West and almost as dark-skinned.

I get a cup of Joe quickly and head over to join him.

"You *are* okay meeting here, Josh?" checks Father Ben.

I glance around at the cafe, out at the street, with the tall buildings towering overhead. I didn't enjoy walking here, but...

"My city-phobia really ain't so bad, now, after all that time inside."

Father Ben nods. "Good. Well, the Lord does delight in bringing good out of bad."

I shrug. "I dunno if it'll last. But I'm okay here today."

"Good enough."

"Darryl and Harry okay?" I check.

"Yes."

I lower my voice. "No one suspicious about Maurice?"

"I don't think so. They had a touching reunion

with their dad at the hospital, with the police looking on. It would have fooled me. Darryl seemed a bit strained, I guess, but if I hadn't known her from a babe in arms, I wouldn't have noticed anything."

My turn to nod. "Can't blame her. I guess it's easy to know in her head that he didn't come back to them 'cause of the depression, but harder to believe it in her heart. I hope Maurice don't get in trouble, anyways. He don't deserve it. Their dad were swearing blind he would get Maurice sent to jail for kidnapping him — which Maurice didn't do."

"Keeping someone locked up for two years is still pretty serious, though."

"Oh, come on. Maurice musta spent big bucks buying Mr. Franklyn from Seb. To *save his life*. He don't belong in jail. Seb, on the other hand. And that Martin Selman guy who hired Seb..."

"It's going to be hard for William, coming to terms with the fact that his new wife's brother did this to him. And by doing it, indirectly caused her death."

"Don't suppose they've arrested him?"

"Martin Selman?" Father Ben shakes his head ruefully. "No. And you know it's unlikely they will. Not on the evidence of one anonymous note. The most we can hope is that they keep a closer eye on him from now on. Maybe they'll catch him doing something else."

I sigh. "I sure hope so. We ain't got nothing at all

on Seb. And I can't help thinking it's only a matter of time before he does some'at bad again."

"Unfortunately, you're probably right. But no evidence is no evidence."

"Yeah. Well, as long as he stays away. Oh, yeah…" I tell Father Ben all about Seb's arrival last night, and how I had to talk nice to him all evening and watch him schmoozing my friends. "But he's gone," I conclude eventually, making Father Ben's frown finally ease. "Left bright and early this morning. So bright and early, I guess he were on his way somewhere."

"Well, I think you're wise to stay as far away from him as you can."

"You're telling me!"

"Anyway," Father Ben checks the time, "we'd better talk about the burial. There are some preliminary forms and things to fill out. We can do that online, now. Then you need to figure out where and when, and there'll be one final form."

"Wow. Why is it so complicated? I thought you just buried a guy and then filed a report after."

"Out in the wilds, Josh," says Father Ben gently. "Not in-city."

"But I don't wanna bury him in-city."

"Well, it's illegal to just bury someone randomly in the middle of nowhere unless circumstances mean it's impractical to bring them in-city to the coroner."

"Yeah, but thanks to the city-folk, I ain't burying a body. Just a jar of ash!"

"It still counts as human remains. To bury them out-city, you need a registered site."

"Like where?"

"Most hunter camps register a burial plot. Many farms do, too."

"Really? Huh. West and the others just set up their own camp. Well, I should say *Ed* and the others, really, since he's the camp boss. Though I doubt he's doing much bossing."

"Would they let you bury him there?"

"Mebbe. I can ask them. Dunno if they have a plot registered yet, though."

"You could deal with that for them. That would be fair."

"I guess." I must sound unenthusiastic, because Father Ben grins.

"It's not that complicated, Josh. I can help you."

"Everything to do with city-folk is 'that complicated.'" I make air quotes. "But yeah, if it gets Wilhelm a place and helps Technicolor, I'll do it, sure. Better to get it done now than have to do all that when Thiago's dear old mom finally...y'know."

"Good. Well, let's fill in the forms we can fill in now, then I have to get going." He pulls out a hand-pad and opens a Net window. "Here. It's straightforward enough."

We work on the forms for a while. We're about done when rapid movements draw my gaze to the doorway.

Cops spill into the cafe, converging on...us.

On me. They're looking at me!

"Joshua Wilson?"

My chair screeches back as I shove away from the table. Are they gonna take me back to jail? No...!

Father Ben wraps me in a bear hug, stopping my lurch to my feet with his superior strength. "Josh, sit down!"

The cops all have a hand on the guns in their holsters...

"He's got a serious phobia of cities and confinement, you've read that in his file, right?" Father Ben is speaking very quickly, but I can barely take it in.

So much for my city-phobia being better. My chest's heaving, I can't breathe. I fight, fight, fight to keep hold of myself. But...

"I ain't going back to jail!"

"We're not taking you to jail, we just want to ask some questions," says one officer.

And if they don't like the answers...

They'll take me back to jail.

Adrenaline floods my body. I gotta get away... I heave against Father Ben, trying to get free. His arms tighten, biting into me painfully.

"Just cuff him to me, would you? I'm serious, *do it*

now!"

And before I know what's happening, one of the cops snaps a handcuff onto my wrist—and onto Father Ben's too.

I tug helplessly at the restraint as he slowly eases his grip on me. "What are you *doing*?"

"Saving your life, maybe. Now, sit down, and let's find out what they want."

Still fighting for breath, I sag back into the chair, just barely clinging to the awareness that if I throw a total crazy fit like I did when I were first imprisoned, I'll probably break Father Ben's wrist or worse.

"I...I ain't done nothing."

"Nobody's said you've done anything," persists Father Ben. "But they clearly need to speak to you."

"That is correct," confirms the senior-looking officer who put the handcuffs onto us. "We just need you to tell us, Mr. Wilson, where you were at ten AM this morning."

"Ten...this morning?" I stare at him, then peer at the time on Father Ben's hand-pad. "You mean, about an hour and a half ago?"

"Yes."

"Uh..." I know it's an easy question, but with panic still fizzing around my mind in little flashes and spurts, it takes me a while to marshal my tongue, and then my confusion simply escapes as, "If you know where I am anyways, why'd you need to ask?"

The cop just smiles thinly. "We only know where you are *now* because you just signed and filed a public form from a device connected to this cafe's NetLink."

I glance at Father Ben's hand-pad. Nosy city-folk.

"So, I ask you again, Mr. Wilson, where were you at ten o'clock?"

Okay, so I guess they do need to ask me. "Uh, ten, I were just arriving here. No, I were slightly late. Got here about three, four minutes past. So I guess...I were walking along that street out there."

Father Ben nods. "I was here when he arrived."

"What time was that?"

Father Ben also bends to consult the treacherous hand-pad, though he swipes through to a messaging program with his free hand. "When he entered I was working on a message, and I sent it while he was waiting for his coffee. At...ten-oh-four. So he probably came through the door about ten-oh-three."

Most of the tension goes out of the senior officer and he glances at what must be his right-hand man. "It's physically impossible for him to have gotten from there to here in that time. This isn't our man."

"So...you ain't gonna put me in jail?" I ask hopefully.

"No."

Relief floods me at his words, almost stealing my breath. But I don't relax entirely. The cop's still there, tapping a thumb to his belt in a thoughtful manner as he eyes me. After a moment, he pulls out a hand-pad of his own and swipes at the screen for a few moments before holding it out to me.

"Mr. Wilson, do you know this man?" His gaze fastens on my face like a night-scope on maximum.

I take the hand-pad with my free hand and look at the picture, while Father Ben leans to peer over my shoulder. Pale skin, brown hair, a city-guy, from the glimpse of collar. And dead, most likely, from his wide, blank eyes and slack mouth, though it's hard to be positive from a still image.

"Never seen him in my life."

"Sure?"

Dutifully, I scan the face again, then shake my head. "Don't know him. He dead?"

The cop reaches in to zoom out on the photo.

"Oh yeah. He's dead," I say, showing Father Ben. There's a round, bloody hole in his shirt right over his heart. Not enough blood for the bullet to have deflected in some bizarre way, missing the heart and leaving him badly injured but alive and bleeding. He died on the spot. And from the size of the hole...

"Rifle?" I ask the cop. "But why in Saint Des's name look at me? Every farmer and hunter in the state has a rifle this kind o'caliber."

"The man's name is Martin Selman. Do you recognize that name?"

I feel my face freeze, my shoulders freeze, every

part of me freezes.

Because as soon as I hear the name, I know who did this. Martin Selman was the only person who could give first-hand evidence against Seb. Seb musta left at dawn, driving through the city-gates to provide himself with a rock solid alibi, then smuggled himself back in-city...

"Yes, you know the name," says the cop, still watching me like a velociraptor watching a rabbit. "But not the face."

Father Ben's gone pretty still beside me, but mebbe he has a better poker-face than me because the cop ain't paying him no attention. My mind over-revs like a 'Vi stuck in the mud. I can't hide that I know the name. Probably can't hide the turmoil the revelation of the dead man's identity has thrown me into. I need to explain why without revealing knowledge of an anonymous note the police ain't made public yet.

"The man's the brother of Darryl and Harry's step-mom," I say. "I dunno what they told you 'cause I weren't allowed to communicate with them for almost a year and we ain't caught up much yet, but I know we'd concluded he were the only person who had any motive to kill or kidnap their dad. We had no evidence, so I dunno if they named him to you guys or not. But I never met him, nor even seen him, no." I glance at the slack face on the screen, then scowl at the cop. "And I sure didn't kill him. What d'you take me for?"

"If there's a motive, we have to check," says the cop blandly. "With motive, means, and opportunity, and a crime like this, we have to check urgently."

I give him one more scowl, then try to stop. My head gets what he's saying, but the rest of me is furious.

"Any idea who might have done it?" asks the cop, and my anger washes away in an icy wave of fear.

Seb. Did he do this because he heard William Franklyn were still alive? Or was this always what he planned to do? Considering that Martin Selman would never have said one word about having hired an assassin to kill someone unless he were already in big trouble and trying to make some deal or put some of the blame onto someone else, that seems stupid. Unless Seb figured Selman were the type to get himself in trouble. And once William Franklyn popped up again alive, well, that greatly increased the chances the police would be asking Selman questions.

Guess Seb don't wanna go back to jail, neither.

I glance at the cop. He still watches me intently. "Mr. Franklyn's okay?" I check. Only reason for Seb to hurt him would be to finish what he were paid to do. But since he's just offed his employer...he's probably heading out-state, with no intention of seeking that kind of work around here again.

"He's fine. We've placed a guard on his room at the hospital, though."

No, Seb has no reason to hurt Darryl and Harry's dad. With Selman dead, there's no evidence of what he did before. William Franklyn never saw nothing, and Wilhelm is dead.

"Mr. Wilson," says the cop. "I'm asking you again. Do you know who did this?"

Yes, I want to say. *I know exactly who did this*. But if Seb learns that I ratted him out to the police...my life won't be worth a rotten hide.

But...Seb's done this right inside the city. So many cameras, so many eyes, fingerprints...won't Seb have missed something? Mebbe he's finally done something the police can actually get him for.

"He obviously knows who did it," says the junior officer, making his superior flap a hand at him again in a "patience" gesture.

"Josh?" Father Ben leans forward to meet my eyes questioningly.

"Should we be asking *you*, Father?" says the cop.

Father Ben just carries on looking at me. Evidence. This time, won't there be evidence? Anyway, I gotta tell, right? Seb ain't gonna stop, ain't gonna turn off this thorny path—and the cops are gonna be mad if I keep silent.

But I really, really, really wanna be able to look Seb in the eye—if I ever have the misfortune to have to— and tell him that I didn't give his name to the cops.

My mouth is dust dry when I open it. I try to

moisten my lips—but my tongue is so dry it don't help much. "I don't know who did it." Not a lie, right? I don't *know*-know. "You'll have to ask me something easier. Mebbe, uh, what's the food like in Exception Central Prison? Bad. Or, uh, which bus did I take this morning? Number 301. Or, uh..." The junior officer scowls, opening his mouth, but the officer silences him with another hand wave, his gaze remaining intent on me. I plow on, "Or, uh...how early did the first HabVi leave the 'Vi-park this morning? Real early. Before dawn, if you must know. One 'Vi, one occupant. Or, um, what coffee did I have before you guys barged in? A—"

"Who. Did. It?" explodes the second cop.

I stare at the dead face on the hand-pad, and don't answer. I don't need to answer. They ain't that dumb, are they?

"Leave it," says the boss cop. "Can't you see the kid's scared? But not stupid. Just contact city gate control and find out who was in that HabVi."

The junior cop pauses for a moment, mouth opening slightly, flushes red from collar to helmet as it clicks, then moves away, speaking into his communicator.

And then, wonder of wonders, the cop is taking the hand-pad and holstering it. The other cop unlocks the handcuffs. Cops three and four have already disappeared outside. Are we free to go?

"I just need the two of you to confirm your contact details, and that's all for now."

"I'm going out-city later today," says Father Ben, "and I'm sure Josh needs to head out as well."

Especially after this, I can hear him thinking, and he ain't wrong. I ain't gonna drive right off to Technicolor's new camp and leave Darryl and Harry until their dad's out of hospital, but after this, I'm heading outside that suffocating fence for tonight, at least.

At least...I listen breathlessly for the cop's reply...I really, really hope I am.

"As long as we have your contact details, that's fine. We may need to talk to you in more detail, Mr. Wilson, about the person you didn't name to us. But it's likely that it won't be necessary."

Won't be necessary? Because there'll be enough other evidence? I sure hope so.

+

Boy, am I glad to get off that bus and walk the final stretch to the 'Vi-park! I'm gonna drive out-city right now. I'll park myself on the bluff in line with the 'Vi-park so I can see through my binoculars if Darryl and Harry come visit, and head back in.

Yeah. I'll eat my lunch once I'm free of this fence. My phobia ain't come back quite the way it used to be, but it ain't as dormant as it has been.

I tap the doorpad to open it and vault up into the

'Vi. But the lights are on. I look around.

Darryl and Harry sit in chairs, eyes focusing on me. But even as my heart starts to lift, I register how stiffly they're sitting. That they're not rising to greet me. That they're...very uneasy. That...I sense another presence, just before…

"Hello again, cub."

I spin the rest of the way around. Seb stands in the rear corner, his rifle held casually in such a way that he could point it at any one of us with only a twitch of his hands.

My heart accelerates like a stampeding herd of triceratops, smashing against my ribs hard enough to hurt. With the most immense effort, I attempt to hide my fear and act normal. I left even my hunting knife in the 'Vi when I headed to the cafe earlier, out of consideration for the city-folks' delicate feelings…

"Seb! You startled me. Thought you left this morning." Darryl and Harry's eyes widen, at the name. Trying to distract Seb from noticing their reactions, I hurry on, "Did anyone get you a cup of Joe? I'm gonna have one."

I step casually toward the kitchen area. If I can open the drawer, there's a sharp knife—

Seb's rifle twitches up, pointing straight at me. "*Ah-ah-aah*, cub. Don't even think about it."

"About coffee?" I attempt to look puzzled. "You

shouldn't be pointing that at me, Seb, your safety catch ain't on. I know you're a city-born and all, but that really is lax."

"Very funny, cub." But there ain't a trace of humor in Seb's eyes now as he stares at me.

Every muscle in my body knots up, tighter than tight, as though that'll help stop a bullet. He's already killed Martin Selman. What's it to him if he kills me too?

"You ain't getting your share of the 'Vi back," I say quickly. "I have a will too, y'know—and you ain't in it."

I have to stop him. Somehow. If he does it in front of Darryl and Harry...he'll kill them too, won't he? In fact...

"I don't know what you're talking about, cub," purrs Seb. "But then, you always were a crazy one. I just need a lift out-city. I'm sure you'll oblige."

Yeah... I swallow. Darryl and Harry have seen him, here, in-city, where he ain't supposed to be. I'm guessing it's pure chance they were here when he turned up—but he ain't gonna let any of the three of us live to talk about it, is he?

"And"—Seb's eyes bore into mine, no doubt reading far too much fear in them—"I reckon you already know why."

DARRYL

"I don't know what you're talking about," mutters Josh.

Every second I observe Josh, the harder my heart pounds and the more the hair prickles coldly up my back. Because Josh is scared. Really scared. Josh, who'll face down a T. rex without breaking a sweat. Leaving aside all the city-phobia stuff, the last time I saw Josh this scared, we were cornered on a roof by a criminal who was gonna shoot us all.

O God, help us! Josh thinks this Seb guy is gonna kill us.

I want to think I'm overreacting, but I can see it in every tense line and tendon of Josh's face and body. We're in more danger than we've ever been in.

I glance at Harry, whose face still shows unease instead of outright fear. How can I protect him?

"Sure you do," sneers Seb. "Police had a little word with you, did they? Like you'd have it in you."

Josh says nothing. Police? What?

Seb gives his head a slight jerk, as though giving up on getting Josh talking. "So. Here's how it's gonna be. You take me out-city, and I'll thank you nicely and we'll go our separate ways."

Harry relaxes slightly, relief on his face.

Josh doesn't relax even the tiniest bit. "If you're in trouble with the police, Seb, you should just give yourself up. It'll be better in the long run."

Seb shifts the gun slightly, so it's pointing straight at me. My chest goes so tight and funny, it's stopping me breathing right. This guy is a murderer — or as good as. "Or you can take me out-city?"

"Fine, fine!" Josh holds up his hands, palms open, then turns slightly toward the cab.

"*Ah-aaah.*" Seb stops him. "*Here's* how it's gonna be. The young cub and I will be in the freeze-drier, safe from the heat scanners. You and your little mare will be in the cab. And if I have the slightest suspicion you're playing me dirty" — he takes one hand from the rifle, other finger resting dangerously on the trigger, and touches the big hunting knife at his belt — "I'll slit the boy's throat, all nice and quiet. So unless you want a nasty sight when you open that freeze-drier up again, you'll make very sure no one is suspicious."

My heart feels scrunched up, malfunctioning, and my skin has gone ice-cold as I stare at my little brother.

Seb grips the rifle two-handed again and jerks the tip at Harry. "Up and in, cub."

HARRY

Is this guy serious? He doesn't really think he can just hold us up in Josh's 'Vi, right here in the city?

"Leave Harry alone." Darryl's voice is thin and strained. "I'll be your hostage."

Josh winces, his eyes darting from Darryl to me

like he doesn't know which idea he likes the least.

"I'm holding the gun, doll, so I get to pick." Seb jerks the gun at me again. "In."

I glare at him. "You'll never get away with—"

"Harry, get in the freeze-drier." Josh sounds tenser than I've ever heard him. Like he's real scared, and Josh is barely scared of anything.

Stomach fluttering uncomfortably, I open the freeze-drier door and squeeze inside. It's almost empty—guess Technicolor cleared out the old packs of food, and Josh hasn't had time to refill it yet. There's just room for Seb to squeeze in as well. Placing the naked knife blade to my throat, he uses his free hand to wedge his rifle like a barrier between me and the door before gripping me firmly across the chest to hold me in position. Immediately, I feel a desperate need to swallow, though it makes the razor edge scrape against my skin.

"Listen up, you two." Seb's voice is sleek in my ear. "If I hear the tiniest sound that might suggest that gun cabinet is being opened—the kid dies. If I have the slightest suspicion you're tipping off the authorities in some way—the kid dies. And if you give the game away by accident by acting too tense—well, tough jerky, the kid dies. Got it?"

"No tricks," says Josh in a low voice. "We got it."

Darryl nods silently. They both stare at me, eyes twin pools of terror in the bright interior lights—and suddenly I'm scared too. Really scared.

Darryl sees it, 'cause that fear—almost—leaves her eyes as she cranks a reassuring trying-to-be-a-smile onto her face.

Then the closing door hides their faces—and it's just me and Seb and the knife, in the dark.

DARRYL

As soon as the door is closed, I glance at Josh and point at the gun cabinet, questioning him with my eyes. He shakes his head sharply.

Oh yeah. What did he say once, that in all his years living in this thing, he and his dad never managed to get their .22s out in the morning to shoot rabbits without clinking or clanking and waking his uncle— who slept in the cab. Far, far too much chance Seb will hear us.

Josh darts to the console—is he gonna send a message to someone?—but with a wary glance at the freeze-drier, he swiftly types in a code, then turns towards the cab as the screen goes blank. Oh. I bet he's just locked down all the 'Vi's computer systems, to block Seb from getting in them.

Josh is already going through the door into the cab on the left-hand side of the living area. He slides through the gap between the driver's seat and the long bed-seat that takes up the rest of the vehicle's width, then settles into the driver's seat and turns the key. I hurry into the cab too, and with the engine running, I dare to whisper to him. "What are we going to do?"

Josh shoots me a look, his eyes a little wild. "Right now, we drive out-city without alerting anyone, so Seb don't kill Harry."

"And then?"

Josh grimaces, pressing the gas and pulling away very, very gently. Thinking of that blade pressing to Harry's throat? My stomach feels like I've swallowed all the ice off a frozen lake.

"Will he let us go once we've done what he wants?" I persist.

Josh hesitates for a long, long moment as he eases the 'Vi through the 'Vi-park gates, and I'm pretty sure he's fighting the temptation to lie to make me feel better.

"No," he murmurs, at last. "He pretended to leave the city this morning, then he smuggled himself back in and shot Martin Selman dead."

"He what?" Just barely, I keep my voice low.

"Mebbe he was gunning for me, anyways, but now you and Harry have seen him here in-city too. He ain't letting none of us go."

"Then why are we doing as he said?"

"Because right now, we just gotta make sure he don't kill Harry. The more time we buy, the more chance we'll get an opportunity."

"Should we jump him as soon as we get out-city, and he's out of the freeze-drier?"

"Only as a last resort. Three of us, we'll probably take him, sure, but at least one of us will die."

And that one will probably be Josh, the one Seb will see as most dangerous and shoot first. All the same...my icy guts clench. "But what if we wait, and he...he offs us the moment we're out-city?"

"And risks the gunshots being heard, and the bodies found? He ain't gonna do it that quickly. Most likely he'll wanna drive well into the wilds before he makes his move. Make sure the evidence will be et up before no one can find it."

"But...why kill Selman? Guess he was the only one who could give first-hand evidence against him, right? But why come after you? 'A dead man told me' isn't going to be worth anything in court."

"Together with Selman's testimony, what Wilhelm told me mighta carried some weight. Seb's made sure that ain't gonna happen, though, so mebbe it's just paranoia. Or spite. Or he hopes I don't really have a will, and the government will offer him my share back at market value on an easy payment plan."

"That's what they do?" I ask the question automatically, though I've never felt less interested in the fate of HabVis whose owners die without a will.

Josh nods, like he doesn't feel very interested either, cruising along the in-city ring-road as though we're carrying a heavy cargo of delicate and priceless eggs.

"So our plan is...?"

"We wait for our chance. And we don't jump him too soon."

"Or one of us will die," I say grimly.

And it'll probably be Josh.

JOSHUA

I spare a glance for Darryl. "Sit and get your belt on. We *cannot* get pulled over."

I hear rather than see her swallow hard, and she plunks down on the seat at once, fumbling for the seatbelt with shaking hands.

Was I right to tell her everything? Yeah. She has to know the stakes. I am absolutely one hundred percent sure that Seb has no intention of letting any of us live.

Saint Des, pray for us!

We just need a moment's distraction and then— there's three of us. We'll have a good chance.

But Seb knows that. What if he knocks us all on the head or tranks us as soon as we get out-city? Then he can drive as far as he likes before shooting us and chucking us out. Or just cutting us a little and leaving us for the carni'saurs, like he originally planned for Darryl and Harry's dad.

Very cold. Very clean. Very...not Seb. If he didn't

know us and it were just business, sure. But Seb don't like me one bit. He's gonna want to look me in the eye when he kills me. Gonna try and make me cower and beg. Yeah, he's gonna keep us awake and enjoy watching us sweat. But he'll be very, very vigilant.

That limits how far he can take us to however long he can remain awake and alert. But he could easily take us three or four hours into the wilderness. When you're hunting, stake-out shifts run that long, and longer.

But the wilderness ain't the danger. Seb is.

My attention shifts to the city-gate, now coming into view ahead.

"I know it's easier said than done, but we gotta be calm."

"Yeah, I know." Darryl mops her face on her sleeve and rolls her shoulders, stretching her mouth and jaw as she tries to relax her face and body. Then, in a smaller voice, she asks, "He'll really kill Harry?"

"I reckon so. Probably enjoy it."

Darryl swallows hard again, like she's feeling queasy, and mops her face once more. "Right. Right. Let's...let's talk about something...normal."

"Yeah. Good idea. I saw West, Trudi, and Ed last night." I pull gently to a halt at the end of the line for the gate.

"Thiago okay?" she asks.

"Yeah, he's trying to get the camp in shape before

I show up, I reckon."

"Isn't Ed the camp boss? Why didn't he stay behind?"

I snort, easing the 'Vi forward as the car ahead moves. "Ed is not the person to leave doing urgent chores. He's so laid back, he's only just finishing off that house he's building for his sweetheart. Y'know, the house he started building just after we got dragged in-city a year ago?" Forward again...

"Well, if he's been out hunting half the time..."

"It's just a two-room cabin with lean-to amenities." Ease to a halt again. "He bought a truck-load of planks ready-cut, the lazy-bones. And he's got plenty of willing hands helping him."

"Okay, so a year is real slow. She, uh, still waiting for him, then?"

"Sounds like. Guess it's good that she's so patient, if she's gonna marry Ed."

DARRYL

"Don't be mean," I tell Josh.

He shoots me a surprised look. "I weren't. I mean it. Once all the gooey feelings wore off, Ed and an impatient woman would be clashing soon enough. Or she'd be getting mad at him, leastways."

"I guess." I stare at the gate as Josh moves us forward yet again. A cop car sits there. Guess there'll be one on every gate after a murder.

"Apparently he's only got the anti-climb metal sheathing to put on the outside walls now," Josh tells me, managing to speak almost normally, "and it's done. Fitted the allo-proof windows the other week."

"That's good."

An aching silence falls as I rack my brains for something else to say. But a horrible thought comes into my head. "You are free to leave the city, right? What did Seb mean about you and the police?"

"They surprised Father Ben and me at the cafe, but they're happy I had nothing to do with the murder, and they said straight out I'm allowed to go out-city."

I relax slightly. We cannot be stopped. We can't. Harry with a knife to his throat... I try to push the image away. I can't let it get to me. I'm sweating again, despite the ice shards filling my stomach.

"Uh, so, is Thiago gonna find himself a lady, now he has a fence to offer her?" I'm proud that I remember the hunter phrase.

Josh is silent for a moment or two. "Well," he says at last, "nothing's impossible. But I reckon not."

"No?"

"Not every man wants to marry. Thiago puts his faith and his friends before anything like that."

I've a feeling that if I spoke completely fluent Hunter-ese, I'd understand what Josh is telling me. As it is, I just wonder slightly.

The car ahead is stopping at the barrier. I grope for words, for calm.

"That's, uh, good, I guess?"

"Yeah. It's a good choice."

The ice churns slightly, despite everything. What's he saying? That he thinks not marrying is a good choice?

Josh shoots me a glance. It's hard to tell with his warm tan skin, but I think he's blushing. "I mean...for him. It's a good choice for him, y'know?"

Possibly. I possibly know. But I don't like to pry and...and we're moving forward again.

O Lord, help us!

HARRY

Seb's knife presses against my throat as we draw to a halt yet again. He has it turned so the cold flat of the blade chills my skin, to avoid slitting my throat simply by accident, I guess, but the tiniest twist of his wrist would ram the razor-sharp edge into me. I'm breathing too fast as I try to keep hold of myself. I don't want Seb to know how scared I am.

But the 'Vi bumps over a pothole and the knife tilts slightly, the edge slicing through the top layer of my skin, sharp, searing pain, and suddenly I'm shaking and I can't stop. If he drove that knife even a little further in...

My stomach wants to heave. I fight to control it. If I let that happen, I'll probably slit my *own* throat.

I hate that Seb can feel me trembling. I *hate* it.

Aren't we almost at the gate?

But what will happen next? I figured Seb would let us go, like he said—until I saw Darryl and Josh's faces.

A drop of liquid drips onto my neck from Seb. Sweat? Guess he's pretty tense, despite trying to act so cool.

Josh once said that scared people do really stupid or bad things, sometimes. And I don't reckon Seb's too bothered about doing bad things at the best of times.

My neck hurts. My head hurts. I can't stop shaking.

Saint Des, I really want my neck to stay in one piece. Pray for me, please!

JOSHUA

The gate official takes my ID and Darryl's, and scans them.

"Anyone else in the vehicle?"

"No." It's a flat-out lie, but this has to count as being under duress.

He glances at the thermal camera screen to confirm what I said, then scans the two cards. My heart clenches as he suddenly double-checks something on the screen—no, breathe, it's probably my parole status, and I've been granted 'electronic sign-in only' due to my 'itinerant lifestyle.' Yes, he hands the cards back and presses the gate button.

The barrier swings up.

Fighting not to heave a big, obvious sigh of relief, not to hurry in a suspicious manner, I ease off the hand brake and gently press the gas. And we're through.

Now what do we do?

DARRYL

"I've been thinking," says Josh suddenly—and very quietly—as we drive on along the highway. "Any chance you or Harry see to get out of the vehicle, you take it, okay? Tell Harry if you get a chance. Any of us see a chance, we go. Don't wait for the others."

"I can't leave Harry here!" Or you... And like Josh will leave *us*!

"There's a good chance if one of us gets out, the confusion will give the others a chance to get out too."

"You'd abandon your 'Vi to Seb? Your dad's 'Vi?"

Josh's face tightens, eyes pinching with pain. "It ain't worth more than our lives. And if we jump him, the odds of at least one of us dying are just too high. None of us are trained fighters. You and Harry ain't nowhere near as strong as Seb, neither. It's crazy-dangerous. Our odds are better if we simply get away from him. We can handle the wilderness. We can't handle an evil man with a gun bare-handed, and it's crazy to try if we have any other option."

I guess when he puts it like that, he's got a point. "I'll try to tell Harry."

Uh-oh... The sound of the freeze-drier door opening. Almost afraid to look, I peep around the cab doorway into the living area. Two pairs of eyes gleam from the dark interior, both alive and moving.

"You two, show me your hands," comes Seb's voice.

I poke mine around the doorframe, while Josh briefly lifts his from the steering wheel.

"Okay, cub, you can get out." Seb herds Harry out in front of him, pointing the rifle at him again as soon as he has room to.

"Where d'you want me to drop you off, Seb?" asks Josh. Guess he figures it's worth a try.

"Closer to the Yoming border," says Seb. "You don't mind helping me out a bit more, do you?"

"Sure," mutters Josh, like he knows full-well it doesn't matter what he minds.

"Right. I'm gonna sit here." Seb kicks a folding seat into the rear corner and settles into it, so he has as clear a view of whoever is behind the steering wheel as possible. "The Raptor Boy can drive for now," he adds. "You two, in here. Sit over there, on the floor."

I settle with Harry in the front corner of the living area, diagonally opposite Seb. That puts us away from the cab door, and all of us as far away from him as possible, but directly in his line of sight—and fire.

How the heck can we possibly get out? Or even try to jump him? He'll see in an instant if we try to reach the door control. And we've so much distance to cover to reach him. No point pretending to be sick. He won't care.

I wrap my arms around Harry and hold him tight, and he doesn't even object. He's figured out how much danger we're in. No surprise; there's a thin, shallow cut on his neck from the knife, oozing a little blood. The sight makes me want to beat Seb with my bare fists.

If only. What the heck are we gonna do?

HARRY

We drive. And drive. And drive.

One hour. It feels longer. Every minute ticks by more slowly than any minute in my life. The cut on my neck stings and seeps. Doesn't Seb care about the blood smell attracting something dangerous?

A couple of times, Darryl tries to whisper something to me, but each time Seb notices. After he threatens to kill me the next time she speaks, she stops.

Seb has the living area shutters open even though we're traveling, probably so he can keep a closer eye on where we're going and if anything's sneaking up on us that Josh isn't going to warn him about. But from my seat on the floor, I can't see anything but sky. All I can tell, from the position of the sun and Josh's lessons on navigation, is that we're heading roughly west. But I know that anyway.

Finally, Seb has me get up, wipe my neck with an odourControl wipe, and smear a little artificial skin on it. Then he makes me bring him a sandwich, promising to shoot Darryl on the spot if I do anything with the knife other than slice bread and cheese.

I'm taller than my big sis, now, but he's far more wary of her. Should I be insulted?

"Oh, and while you're on your feet," Seb adds, "unlock the console for me, would'ya? Something seems to have happened to it while we were in that nasty box."

I glance into the cab, at the back of Josh's head. Josh happened, I guess.

"Uh…I don't know the code," I say. I've seen Josh input it often enough that I do, kinda, but he's never *given* it to me—so it's not quite a lie.

Seb puts down his sandwich so he can put his second hand back onto his rifle and level it very precisely at Darryl. "Raptor Boy, give the pup the code or I'll shoot your little mare."

Josh's shoulders go even more rigid, but after only a fractional hesitation, he reels off the familiar numbers. I type them in, and the screen glows into life.

I move back toward Darryl.

"Not so fast," purrs Seb. "Raptor Boy, let's have

the master code too."

Even from here, I can see Josh's knuckles whiten on the steering wheel. That code will give Seb administrator-level control of all the 'Vi's computer systems. Using that, he can make this *his* 'Vi, wiping all trace of Josh and his family from the drives.

"One," says Seb, when Josh remains silent, his finger tightening on the trigger. "*Two…*"

I'm opening my mouth to scream at Josh to *give me the code* when Josh starts speaking.

I bend over the console, carefully in-putting the long string of numbers and letters. When I press enter, the screen displays:

ADMINISTRATOR ACCESS ENABLED

Seb rises to his feet, leaning over the table slightly to check the display. I tense. Should I grab for his gun?

Too late. His eyes are already back on me. His mouth curves in a mocking smile. "Too slow, pup," he smirks—and he settles back into his chair, safely on the other side of that barrier-like table.

I glance at the console again, but there's nothing I can do. I don't know how to disable the Administrator mode, and Seb will see if I try to touch it. I move toward Darryl instead.

"Not so fast, little larvae. Make me a cup of Joe, too," Seb orders.

I move back to the kitchen area, moving as slowly as I dare while my mind races. Is *this* my chance? What could I put in it, other than coffee? Something tasteless but harmful? The tranquilizers are in too-obviously a non-food cupboard, and I don't even know if they'd work when swallowed. The cleaning products are mostly natural—and not kept in the kitchen cupboards either.

In the movies, they always have something conveniently at hand, but I can't think of anything. I guess I could fill it with chili and hope he took a big enough first swig that getting a mouthful distracted him just enough. But I don't reckon he's that dumb. He's gonna sniff it and sip it, first.

"D'you really think Mr. Goody Two Shoes keeps any poison in that kitchen cupboard, kid? Hurry up, or you'll be down by one sister."

A wash of cold sweat breaks out all over me. My hands tremble as I fumble with the mug. *Outage*, he knew! How'd he know?

'Cause it's the obvious thing to try, idiot.

I place the mug on the end of the table, like he ordered for the sandwich, not going too close to him. He waits for me to return to the corner before reaching for it. Still shaking, I settle beside Darryl. Her arms go around me again at once. But the way she watches Seb...like a mother raptor watching a larger predator. Yeah, I reckon she'd pull the trigger on Seb, under the circumstances. I hope I would too, but maybe I'd hesitate and get us all killed.

She'd have to get close enough to get the gun, first. Seb eats his sandwich, drinks his coffee, but his eyes shift between Darryl and me, and Josh, back and forth, back and forth. He's not letting his guard down for a moment.

Maybe he also knows what that look in a raptor's eyes means.

JOSHUA

The terrain is so flat and open. I keep looking out for anywhere I could throw the 'Vi out of control, and Seb out of his chair, but there's nothing. I could try a sharp swerve, but it would be far too quick for Seb to make it into the cab and regain control—then pick us off as we ran. Whenever I casually try to take a route that leads to hillier ground, his voice soon comes from behind me.

"*Ah-ah-aah*, cub. Not that way."

Guess it ain't hard for him to figure out what I'm planning.

All the same, we can't get all the way to the Yoming border without getting into hillier country. There's even a mountain range to cross. Eventually, I'll get my chance, right?

Finally...I can see hills ahead. My shoulders tense,

though, back prickling. Will Seb make his move? He's secured all the access he needs to the 'Vi. And we're already far enough into the wilderness that Seb would be real unlucky if anyone found our bodies. But the further we go, the safer he'll be.

"Cub, get back in here. Let your little mare drive now."

Misfire! But does he think Darryl won't try the exact same thing?

She'd better. We're running out of time.

HARRY

Josh stands facing us in our corner once he's come through, not sitting at once, stretching as though stiff after three hours of driving. But...I realize that his one finger, the only part of his hand out of sight of Seb, is moving in a very deliberate way. Slow waves, then fast waves, then slow, slow...

Just in time, it clicks. Morse code! He made us learn it, along with all the other hunter stuff.

Trying not to stare too hard, I watch as he quickly spells out:

CRASH RUN DONT WAIT

Out of the corner of my eye, I see Darryl's face tighten at the last order. Her eyelids shiver down, though, in the tiniest sign of assent, and she rises to her feet.

"On second thought..." Seb's voice makes her tense so hard I guess she's expecting a bullet. "The pup can drive."

"Me?" I say stupidly. Then anger stirs. He's so sure I'm young and wet-behind-the-ears and no threat, isn't he? If only I could prove him wrong.

"Yeah, you. Go on."

I get up and go to the cab doorway, then stop, peering ahead. I almost open my mouth to protest that the country up ahead is hilly—mountains in the far distance—and I shouldn't be at the wheel when I haven't even driven the 'Vi for a year. But I bite my tongue just in time. If I say that I'm not safe to drive, maybe he'll just...do whatever it is he's going to do, right away.

And I don't think any of us want that.

It's not like there's any snow yet. I settle into the driver's seat, but sweat breaks out all over me as Josh's order runs through my mind.

Crash the 'Vi and run. Don't wait for the others.

If Josh is prepared to crash his precious 'Vi...then Seb really is going to kill us.

But I'm just supposed to leave them in here? Leave Darryl here?

I guess the crash will finally give Josh the chance to jump Seb, right? And if I'm out of the vehicle, I'm one less person for him to worry about. Couldn't I help take Seb down, though? Well, maybe not from the cab. By the time I'm up and around the seat and through the doorway and across the room and... I guess it'd all be over by the time I got there, so I'd just be another body for flying bullets to find.

So—I start the engine, pull forward—am I going to obey? It's Josh's 'Vi, he's the boss. Well, technically, I don't work for him right now. Didn't even choose to come along on this trip. All the same...if I trust anyone to figure out our best chance of getting out of this, it's Josh.

However much I hate the thought of leaping out without knowing if they'll be okay...Josh must have his reasons for demanding it. He'll have weighed the odds, the way hunters do, and this is the safest option.

Just so long as I can actually bring myself to go, when the moment comes.

DARRYL

Josh sits close beside me, his body a welcome line of warmth down my side. Despite the tension, I've been sitting still for hours now, and the day is cold. I'd already taken my coat off when Seb came to the door; he won't let me get it to put it back on, and I'm freezing. And, honestly? I'm really scared.

Once, Josh slips his hand into my hand, his fingers

giving mine a warm, welcome embrace—but Seb notices almost immediately.

"Hands where I can see 'em, cub," he snaps.

Josh returns his hands to his knees. After a while, our heads drift together instead, bumping gently as the 'Vi rocks over the rough ground.

Is Harry going do what Josh told him to do? I guess there must be hillier country coming up, finally, and that's why Seb made Josh switch. I'm glad Harry may have the best chance of getting out of the vehicle—but I'm scared Seb will shoot him if he figures out what he's about to do. I almost wish I was driving. But that would mean leaving Harry in here with Seb...

This situation is awful and impossible.

And it's getting worse. More and more often, Seb takes an extra moment to look at me. Just a lingering fraction of a second extra before his eyes move on to Josh and to Harry and to Josh and back to me—*linger*—and to Josh and to Harry, on and on and on...

Exactly what is he planning?

And how much longer can he be bothered to keep this up?

JOSHUA

I watch Seb eyeing Darryl, my teeth clenching so hard I hear them grind together. Does he plan to shoot me and Harry first? The thought drives me wild, fury and adrenaline rushing through me, but there ain't nothing I can do. Yet.

Worse, what if he puts us out of the 'Vi and drives off with Darryl? No, he wouldn't drive off. He'd cut Harry and me and then watch until we'd been et up. Make Darryl watch? My stomach churns.

No, he won't do that, will he? He must be in a real hurry to get across that border. Sure, you can be extradited for murder—but Seb will find someone to give him a new identity—my 'Vi a new identity, too— and he'll be off scot-free.

So whatever he does, it won't be slow. And he won't leave me alive out here. Anyone else, mebbe, but not me. He knows my reputation too well, knows that if anyone were gonna be so annoying as to walk out of the wilderness alive to tell tales, it would be me.

So it's probably gonna be a bullet.

If he looks like he's gonna make his move, I'm gonna try to jump him. What else can I do?

If he had any sense, he'd just suddenly shoot me, without a word to betray his intent. But he's gonna want to watch me squirm. And it ain't gonna make no difference, is it? The distance between us—yet again I measure it with my gaze, picturing the time to rise, the time to move, to dodge around the table—it's just too much.

At least if he decides to keep Darryl till last, she might get a better chance to take him out. She might just be the one to survive. It's a thin hope fraught with horrible risk, but at least it's a hope. Barely.

Come on, Harry. Everything's resting on you now.

But we've got to reach the slopes first. If Harry tries something too soon, Seb will just shoot him, or pick us off as we run, and it'll all be over.

Be patient, Harry. It seems like Seb is determined to get as far as possible before dispatching us. So choose your moment and make it count.

HARRY

Finally, we're climbing up into the first foothills of the distant snow-tipped mountains. Seb gives occasional orders about what route to take, and I make sure to obey very precisely, giving no hint of drifting off course the way Josh was often doing.

I'll only have one chance. He's got to think I'm being a good little cub.

Up a valley we go, down another. Up again. But the gradients are too gentle. Deeper and deeper into the hills. Deeper and deeper. Occasionally, a light sprinkle of snow dusts a shady slope, high above us. But we stay down in the smooth valleys. Still nothing. How long will he wait?

My back prickles as though icy fingers are stroking down it. Will he shoot me first, while I'm driving? No, he'll shoot poor Josh first. Then Darryl, right?

Darryl....

Or will he shoot *me*?

Another cold rush sweeps over me. *No, no, no...* How can I jump out and *leave* her?

But Josh...Josh must be desperate to get her away from Seb. If he thinks this is the best way...

I've gotta do it.

But where?

Saint Des, Lord, Mother Mary, Mom, please, please, please?

JOSHUA

Seb glances out of the window more frequently now. Eyeing the terrain? Or checking for signs of scavengers? Is he looking for the best spot to dump our bodies?

Come on, Harry!

We're almost out of time. I'm near-certain. If Harry can make a sharp turn to the left, he'll send Seb flying across the living area—but Darryl and I are already up against the side door. All we need to do is straighten and push the button and we're out. *If* Harry can find somewhere to do it.

If he can't...then any moment now, Seb's gonna make his move. I clench and relax my muscles, trying to loosen them after driving and now sitting for so long, try to get them as ready as I can for a desperate lunge across the living area. I feel Darryl doing the same beside me.

Maybe, just maybe, in the time it takes Seb to shoot me, she can reach him.

And overpower him? How?

I clench my fists, furious with helplessness.

Then, with effort, I try to relax them.

Lord? Take care of us, please?

One way or another.

DARRYL

I can see Seb's increasingly restlessness; I can feel Josh preparing himself. I try to do the same, but my heart pounds harder and harder, and my stomach churns. In just a few moments, is Josh going to be dead on the floor? And Harry? What will happen to me?

I scan the room again, desperately looking for anything I can use against Seb, if Josh...if Josh manages to...to distract him...long enough. Can I hit him with the empty mug?

Hard enough to knock him out?

Or just hard enough to yank the rifle out of his dazed hands?

He won't let go that easily. Not when his life depends on it.

What if I just...knock him off the chair and kick him? Stamp on his face?

Beat him to pulp with the chair? Yeah. Anything and everything. I gotta do whatever it takes.

For Harry.

Unless... *Harry, come on.*

Lord, please?

HARRY

Seb's shifting more. I can see him in the living area cam. Looking outside, looking at me. Like he's trying to make up his mind when's best to make his move.

My mouth is so dry I can barely moisten it.

Where? Where can I—?

Whoa! We've just crested the innocent-looking slope we've been trundling up—and it drops down steeply on the other side. A long, flat, open slope, yes, with few boulders—but steep. Really steep.

Not allowing myself time to think—not allowing Seb time to get a look at the terrain—I spin the wheel sideways in the direction that will throw Seb across the vehicle, which also points us straight down that incline, and shove the cruise control throttle up to maximum. Seb's rifle fires, but I don't know where the bullet goes. The G-force of our turn makes reaching out a hand harder than it should be, but my fingers close around the door handle—pull—I hurl myself at the door, using my own weight to open it.

Then I'm in mid-air, falling—*oh no, what if the 'Vi runs over me?*—thud, I'm on the ground, so hard, my breath is gone, *air, I can't breathe*! The 'Vi is rushing past me, so close...the side door opens and two figures leap out, rolling as they land and regaining their feet at once.

Josh looms over me; he grabs my shirt, hauls me up. "Run, Harry!"

And he's towing me beside him as I whoop and gasp, my winded body struggling to draw a full breath, agony in my chest.

"Run!" shouts Josh again, as Darryl appears alongside us.

We head sideways across the grassy slope as the 'Vi tears off down the hillside, weaving slightly as it hits bumps. Seb will be too busy trying to regain control to worry about us, right?

"Run," gasps Josh, yet again, dragging me still faster.

I catch a glimpse of distant outcrops ahead. That's where we're headed, right?

"Faster," Josh urges.

The 'Vi's engine still revs wildly as the cruise control attempts to take it to top speed on this rough terrain. My chest burns, my legs burn, and I stagger more and more. *Need. More. Oxygen.*

The rocky area is getting closer...

The 'Vi's engine note changes. The revs drop suddenly.

Seb's reached the cab.

DARRYL

"Run!" yells Josh, more fiercely than ever.

I grab Harry's other arm and tow him as well. From the way he's gasping and wobbling, his breath must have been knocked out of him when he threw himself headlong from the 'Vi like that. Definitely the safest when it came to avoiding being shot right then, but now...

I half tow, half carry him, and Josh does the same.

The 'Vi's engine noise changes again. Turning? Will Seb chase us, or just stop in a good position and pick us off from there.

"Quickly!"

We're almost at the rough ground. Almost...

The revs die right down. Seb's stopping.

"Hurry!" We're passing between rocks at last, but Josh drags us onwards several more strides before finally throwing us all to the ground behind a larger boulder. "Down! Stay down! Do not raise your head! Stay down!"

The urge to look, to see what Seb is doing, is almost overwhelming. But Josh is right.

"Come on!" Josh is already tugging at us as he

crawls away through the scrub. "Stay low. Keep your head down."

Ah, that was why he ran on those few extra steps, despite the risk. Where we are now, we can keep down behind rocks and make our way back to the looming crags. The very first boulders were all alone. We'd have been pinned down, just waiting for Seb to drive up and—

The 'Vi's engine starts again. Yep, he's going to come closer and try to get a shot at us.

"Quickly," hisses Josh, crawling at lightning speed. "Stay low!"

Harry determinedly wriggles along behind him, still gasping and coughing in a way that wrings my heart out.

"Hurry, Harry!" I can't help adding my voice to Josh's. "You gotta *move.*"

Thank Saint Des, he goes a little faster.

The engine gets closer and closer.

Josh keeps pausing to twist onto his back, and eye behind us with frantic calculation—clearly checking Seb's lines of sight, and that we're still in cover.

Finally, when my elbows and knees feel raw and my heart is exhausted from its too-tense pounding, we're wriggling through a gap in two boulders that Josh can barely fit through—but he makes it. Harry slides through so fast Josh must be dragging him— yep, as soon as I thrust my shoulders through, Josh grabs my arms and pulls me clean over the top of Harry, who lies gasping.

"Down," Josh hisses, yet again, but we're behind a high line of boulders here, boulders far too tall for Seb to get a shot over. We're finally safe.

Safe? No 'Vi, no rifles, no hunting knives, no provisions, Josh the only one with even a fall-weight jacket...

Well—safer than a few minutes ago.

HARRY

We lie there, Darryl and Josh gasping and panting almost as much as I am from fear and exertion, listening to the 'Vi as it cruises up and down on the other side of the rocky ground. After only a few moments, though, Josh is up, crouching, peering around.

He moves to the only tree of any size—barely more than an overgrown shrub—and proceeds to ruthlessly dismember it, emerging with the only three decent-sized branches, none much fatter than my thumb. He hands one to Darryl and one to me, then begins rubbing the end of his branch hard on the nearest boulder, smoothing it to...oh, a sharp point. He's making a spear.

I know I should sharpen my branch too, but I'm still shaking violently from all that running and crawling while oxygen-deprived. I need a minute.

"If Seb comes foot patrolling to get us," Josh says after a few moments, "we take him down, okay?" He glances at Darryl, who nods grimly as she works on her own prehistoric weapon.

"With spears?" I query, finally picking up my stick up. The sticks sure aren't big enough to club Seb with.

"If he comes in among these rocks, there's a good chance we can get the drop on him," says Josh.

"And if he doesn't?"

"Then as long as we stay in here, there ain't nothing he can do to us other than drive off."

Since I've been staring at the NavConsole for almost an hour, that idea doesn't leave me as calm as it leaves him. "D'you know how far it is to the nearest road, Josh? Let alone the nearest fenced settlement. Why didn't you jump him?"

"Because he'd probably have won the fight," says Josh bluntly. "Last time I went hand-to-hand with a snake like Seb, it didn't go too well, and Wilhelm ain't here to help this time."

Wilhelm? My hackles automatically rise at the name, although I know he saved Josh's life in the fight Josh is referring to.

"And this way," Darryl backs Josh up, no surprise, "there's a good chance we can all just hike out of here. If anyone can get us back safely, it's Josh, you know that."

"And so does Seb," says Josh, testing the point of his spear, "so he's gonna be real reluctant to drive off and leave us. But he won't want one of these through his murderous throat, neither."

I swallow slightly. By the sound of it, Josh isn't planning on messing around if Seb comes within range. I guess under the circumstances, we don't have any choice. Him or us. And Seb did mean to kill Dad. All the same, the thought of Josh driving that spear through the man's throat—of me driving a spear through him—it makes me feel real weird.

I start rubbing the end of my stick on the nearest rock as well, grinding it smooth. "Think these are strong enough?"

"Better than nothing," says Josh. "So get a point on it, quick as you can."

He makes a few practice jabs with his own spear, then finally takes a very, very quick look through the gap in the rocks, pulling back at once. "Okay, he's just sitting there in the turret, with the windows open. Hoping we'll peek out long enough to give him a shot, I guess. Or trying to decide what to do."

"So, you think he'll foot patrol—or leave?" checks Darryl.

"Leave, eventually. Or...he might try to guess which way we'll go and set up ready to ambush us. That would be the most dangerous thing. We're gonna have to keep a very, very sharp eye on the distant landscape as well as the near-ground and stay in cover as much as we can. And not head for...lemme see. There are two roads and one hunter camp all about equally close. We'd better not make for any of those three. Too obvious. If we pick a road or settlement that ain't too close nor too far, ain't too hard to get to nor too easy—he ain't got much chance guessing right, then."

"We're not heading for the closest?" I ask uneasily.

"Going a little further is safer than being picked off by Seb from half a mile away," says Josh firmly.

"I guess. When do we head out?"

"When Seb clears off. We ain't leaving this nice 'Vi-proof nest of rocks until he's long gone."

So we wait.

JOSHUA

Every few minutes, I move to a different spot to check on Seb, super-quick. To be sure the snake ain't come out of the 'Vi and is even now sneaking up on us.

But Seb stays in the turret. I ain't surprised.

"There's three of us and one of him," I explain to Darryl and Harry, huddling back up to them for warmth as soon as I return. I've taken my jacket off to share it, but it barely stretches around Darryl and Harry. Only one sleeve drapes over my shoulders, but even that's better than nothing. "He knows if he comes in here, he's gonna get his brains bashed out with a rock, or a sharp stick shoved through him. The fact he might manage to shoot one of us in the process ain't gonna be enough incentive, you betcha it ain't."

All the same, when, after what can't be more than half an hour, the familiar purr of the 'Vi's engine splits the silence, I frown. "He's giving up already?"

I peer around at the distant landscape again. Has he spotted high ground from which he thinks he might get a shot in here? Nah, there ain't nothing. And from the rapidly receding engine noise, he's going straight on the way we were going. Heading for the border again.

"Okay, that is weird," I say.

"Is it?" says Darryl. "If he's not gonna come out here..."

"Yeah, but he shoulda waited longer in the hopes one of us would get careless and stare at him for too long. Or that we'd panic and try to head for safety immediately, and give him a chance at us. Him not coming out here, sure, but giving up this quick? I don't get it."

I don't like it, neither. I thought it would take ages for Seb to accept that he were gonna have to leave me for the wildlife and hope for the best. I'd resigned myself to a long, cold wait before we could get moving—this day ain't getting no warmer, and we're at a much higher altitude now. I were the only one wearing a jacket.

I take a few more peeks through the crack as the 'Vi—*my* 'Vi—disappears rapidly into the distance.

"I really think he is going." He's driving in a super-focused way, actually. Like he wants to make as much distance as he possibly can before...what? It will take us the better part of a week to reach civilization, if we move with any kinda caution and stop to find food, water, and something to keep us warmer, which is looking like a necessity—so we won't be sending no one after him no time soon.

It's almost like some'at's spooked him.

But what?

DARRYL

"Ryl?" Harry's voice is small, all of a sudden.

"What?" My eyes flick over his face, anxiously.

"I'm fine, it's just...what is Dad going to think?"

Dad? *Outage*, I've been so one-hundred-percent focused on saving Harry, on keeping all of us alive, I hadn't even thought about—

"It's gonna look like we ran off with Josh, isn't it?" persists Harry. "He'll think we didn't want to go home with him to the farm."

Aw, heck. Harry's right. There's a log at the city-gate of me leaving with Josh. And if Harry's missing, they'll assume we smuggled him out—and they won't even be wrong, technically.

I barely have to turn my head to glance at Josh, we're all cuddled together so tightly for warmth. "Will they realize Seb took us?"

"I don't see why," Josh replies. "Seb's 'Vi must be parked up somewhere out-city. I dunno if he were gonna send someone to retrieve it or if he just thought he'd swap it for mine. But if they find his 'Vi, they'll assume he's hiding somewhere, waiting to get back to it, or that they cut him off and he's made a run for a border. But I don't see why they'd connect him with us three apparently taking off again. Unless they thought we'd gone after him. I mean, Father Ben or the cops from earlier might be suspicious some'at worse had happened, but where would they even look? Ain't none of it gonna happen soon enough to help us, anyways."

I barely keep from muttering a swear word out loud. "Well, as soon as we get back, we can set Dad straight," I tell Harry firmly. "He's gonna have a bad week, but we can't do anything about that. We've got enough to worry about." And he did leave *us* worrying about him for almost *two years*, so—

"*Oh...*" The desolate sound comes from Josh, so quiet I barely catch it, but he's gone rigid against me, and there's something about his tone that snaps my attention to him at once, raising all the hairs down my back.

He's staring at the horizon as though mesmerized, as he rises to his feet like a sleepwalker.

"Hey!" objects Harry. "It's cold!"

But I'm still watching Josh. His chest heaves as he draws deep breaths, his eyes wide with shock and dismay. He looks...he looks *stricken*.

"I am *so, so* sorry," he whispers at last. "We shoulda never left the 'Vi."

"Not left?" I protest. "But you said if we'd stayed, at least one of us would have died!"

"But the other two woulda lived."

HARRY

What? I stare up at Josh, who's looking super freaked out about something as he gazes off into the distance. Darryl rises to her feet, her head turning as she follows his line of sight. She stares hard into the distance as well. After a moment, her cheeks begin to lose their color.

"Is that a...?" she asks Josh.

"Yeah."

"A what?" I demand. "Is that a *what*?" I peer at the gray horizon myself, but it's just a heavy bank of winter cloud, full of snow, probably. Great. But nothing remarkable about it at all, except the faintest purple hue on the very farthest skyline.

Purple...

And Josh and Darryl both look like Seb's standing over us with a rifle, about to shoot...

"Is that...is that a lightning-freeze?" I choke, scrambling to my feet as well.

"That's a killer-chiller, alright," says Josh dully. "There were a minor warning for up in Tana, nothing more. I guess it got worse real fast."

"Is it heading this way?" asks Darryl, her voice strained.

Like it will matter. With one light jacket between us and no source of heat, we can't survive even the edge of one of the terrifying polar vortex storms that have turned Tana state into a summer-farming-only zone, and which occasionally swoop further down to batter Exception and Yoming with ice and death.

No wonder Seb drove off and left us.

We are *dead*.

DARRYL

In response to my question, Josh glances around, checking the wind, checking the cloud movement high above us.

"Yeah," he sighs. "I reckon it's heading right for us."

"That's it, then." Harry tries for a matter-of-fact voice, but it shakes slightly. After a moment, he sinks back to the ground, wraps his arms around his knees, and rests his chin on them as though he figures he may as well stay as warm as he can for now. Maybe he's praying.

Saint Des, help us!

"No, that's *not* it," I say fiercely, fighting the echoey numbness in my belly that wants to agree. "Josh, what do we do? Find shelter? How long have we got?"

Harry snorts. Yeah, like any shelter we can reach in time will be enough. When the eye of the storm arrives, the temperature will plummet at least fifty, maybe even a hundred degrees in mere minutes. Burrowing animals will be deep underground, herds and packs huddled together in shelter—and the old and the weak still won't make it. Frail little humans? They don't survive this, not unequipped like we are. Hunters inside HabVis have died sometimes, if their heater breaks down, despite all their high-tech thermal gear.

But we can't just...give up. I have to save Harry. We have to get back to Dad!

Josh glances from me to Harry, his eyes agonized. He opens his mouth—then says nothing. For a moment, as he stares fixedly at the horizon, I'm afraid he's actually giving in to despair—then I realize that he's thinking. Hard.

Harry just sits and hugs his knees tightly, but I watch Josh. Does he actually have a plan? For all my determined words, I'm astonished.

Yes, because... "Okay," says Josh at last. "I reckon from that sky that we have a good nine hours before that thing actually hits us. The eye, anyway, which is the really deadly part. Here's what we have to do."

He brushes leaves from a patch of ground in front of Harry with his foot, then crouches beside him, using his spear point to make marks in the dirt.

"Here we are. Here's the Yoming border. Between us and the border, here's the mountain range Seb has to cross." Josh marks a long line of triangles. "It's high and mostly impassable terrain. There are only two passes in a hundred miles. And only one is passable with a HabVi. The other only by foot. The foot pass is here."

Josh marks a spot in the mountains almost directly in line between us and the border. "The off-road vehicle pass is way over here." He marks a place to the south. "Seb will have to take that one. Guess he heard a storm warning and that's why he lit out like that, trying to get over before the storm blocks it. But once across, he'll need to come back to his original course to get around this big lake, here. And only then cross the border. So it's far further in a 'Vi than on foot. Plus, he's gonna have to stop to put the snow tracks on the vehicle, which will delay him even more. By the time he gets over that pass, it's gonna be real late. He don't know this terrain, and the storm will be almost on him.

He's gotta stop and hunker down, wait for it to pass. Best stopping place is right here." Josh marks a place just on the other side of the mountains from the foot pass.

"So?" says Harry bleakly.

"So, we run. We run like a killer-chiller is behind us—'cause it is. Straight to the pass, up, over, down. We can make it before the storm. We take the 'Vi back and survive the storm. Then we drive back to your dad."

"Run?" Harry stares at Josh incredulously. "How far?"

"About thirty miles."

"Thirty miles?" Harry echoes. "It's already mid-afternoon. We can't cover that distance—over a mountain range!—in nine hours! In the dark!"

"We can if we don't stop."

"Don't stop? What about terrain inspections? Checking for danger? We're already bleeding! Something will eat us!"

"It might," says Josh bluntly. "But if we stay here, we die for sure. If we can catch up with Seb, we have a chance. Our only chance. Weigh the odds, Harry. We run."

"But...how can you be sure he'll even *be* there?"

"I can't. But it's quite clear on the map that it's the only good place to stop. Most places around there are pretty dicey, especially in a killer-chiller. Very, very high odds he'll be there."

Harry gapes at him, still, and I can't help staring incredulously at Josh too, even while re-wrapping my braid around my neck a little for extra warmth.

Thirty miles? Usually, hunters pause to inspect every new stretch of terrain before venturing onto it—sometimes for quite a few minutes, depending on what they suspect is lurking in the area. That makes foot patrolling—or foot travel—a painfully slow business. Thirty miles would take two days, bare minimum, done safely.

Thirty miles in nine hours? Simply running flat out, with no thought for predators? Up a mountain, through snow, and into the fast-approaching night? "It's our only chance?"

"Yeah."

I swallow. I guess, a few minutes ago, I was sure we had no chance at all. But, apparently we do. That's good, right?

"Come on, Harry." I reach down and grab his hand. "Get up. We need to go."

JOSHUA

After coating ourselves in mud to hide our human smell—and reduce the blood scent from the cuts and scrapes we acquired leaping out and crawling away from the 'Vi—we move. Frustration crawls up my spine like biting ants as we pause regularly to check that we ain't about to stumble into Seb's line of sight.

I don't want to mention it yet and stress the other two out even more, but we have a more pressing deadline than the killer-chiller. With this cloud cover, and the storm approaching, we'll be lucky if we get any moon at all, and none of us have a flashlight. If we can reach the path up to the pass before we lose all the light, I reckon I can lead us over it and down to the stopping place. But I doubt I can find the path in the dark. If we don't make it to the path, we'll have to use my fire-steel cross to make a fire, which could be slow in this cold damp—and make a bunch of torches, too.

But by the time we've done all that, it'll be too late.

And fire will attract the attention of every inquisitive raptor for miles. Dunno if that's good or bad. Depends if you think getting et or getting froze is an easier way to go.

"I thought you said we couldn't stop for *anything*," objects Harry, as I force myself to halt yet again so I can scan the ground ahead for any signs of the 'Vi. "Do we have time for this?

"No, we *really* don't," I say. "But, at this precise moment, we're way more likely to walk into Seb's line of fire than we are to be jumped by a hungry critter. So we check. Weigh the—"

"Yeah, yeah," snaps Harry. "Weigh the odds, I know."

"Chill, Harry," says Darryl, in an impressively calm voice. "Everything's gonna be fine."

"Oh yeah?" snarls Harry. "I'm fifteen, sis, not five! And this isn't anybody's definition of fine!"

Unfortunately, Harry has a point. But...

"Come on, I don't see 'im. Let's move."

HARRY

Our initial speed may have been frustratingly slow, but soon Josh is convinced from the tracks that Seb is well ahead of us—and things get much worse. Pausing only to snap some light evergreen branches from a suitable bush and poke them through our clothes so they stick out all around us like a halo—improvised "frights" to make us look bigger and scarier—we run without stopping. Josh bounds up slopes, over boulders, races downhill, slides through gaps in crags and boulders, scrambles up rocky clifflets... And he expects us to keep up.

"Hurry up, Harry," he hisses down at me, yet again, as he pulls Darryl up a crag behind him.

I stagger up the slope, my chest burning as I drag in breaths. Josh has come out of prison buff as anything—they had exercise bars in the cells, apparently, and a bunch of treadmills on the wings that the hunters took over at least once a day for an hour. And Darryl's been jogging for months to keep herself sane. Guess I've let my fitness go a little too much, though, while in-city.

"Harry," snaps Josh. "Here!"

Wearily, I reach up and let him grab my wrist. He hauls me up the crag much faster than I could have climbed it, and the moment I'm at the top he's off running again, Darryl right behind him. I stumble to my feet and plow after them, feeling like the dwarf in that classic movie we watch with Dad every Christmas.

Dad. What's he going to think if we get eaten or frozen out here?

My chest clenches from a discomfort that has nothing to do with shortness of breath. I could whack Seb on the head with a rock for doing this to us! It will wreck Dad if we die. And worse, he'll think we left him. Voluntarily.

The thought makes my stomach turn over.

Or maybe that's pure exhaustion.

"Harry, hurry up." Josh's voice snaps me from my depressing thoughts. I put my head down and focus on driving my legs into the ground, on and on and on.

I'm wasted on cross-country. We farmboys are natural sprinters. Very dangerous over short distances.

DARRYL

Josh can be merciless when safety is at stake, but he's never been as ruthless as this. He drives us on, and on, and on. That alone is enough to tell me just how tight the timing is going to be.

And getting to the 'Vi before the storm hits is only the first problem. How do we persuade Seb to let us in, and then overpower him?

Even though Seb got the master code, I'm betting Josh has some kind of back-up code for just this sorta situation. So Josh can probably open the doors. But Seb will hear, right? And shoot us. Taking back the 'Vi was hard enough from inside. From outside? It makes getting there in time seem like the easy part.

Does Josh *really* believe we have a chance? Or did he just come up with this plan to give us hope? Give us something to do other than sit and wait to die?

I try to push the bleak thought away. No. Josh weighed the odds, and this is our best chance.

What our odds actually are, though...

I mean, how is Josh even going to lead us over a mountain in the pitch blackness of night? I glance up at the heavy clouds that are speeding dusk. There won't be any light at all, soon. None.

But hasn't he thought about that?

JOSHUA

I pause beside a stream, kneeling to scoop water to my mouth. Ice crackles around the water's edge, between the reeds. The temperature is dropping fast—like the light. The exercise kept us warm for the first hour, but we're all chilling now. But we have to drink.

We've been running for about three hours, and we're not going fast enough. We gotta reach the path before full dark! Clouds still cover the sky, stealing our hope of moonlight. At least it's not snowing yet, although there are more patches of snow underfoot as we head higher into the mountain range. If the wind rises when we get higher up, frostbite will soon be a danger.

Harry's not going fast enough, truth be told. Darryl and I would be making better time on our own. What do we do if he can't keep going? Until we're over that pass, there's absolutely no chance we could get back to him before the storm arrived, even if we did re-take the 'Vi.

Are we gonna have to choose between staying and dying with him, or leaving him behind to pursue our slim chance of survival? *Would* Darryl even leave him? Would I?

As long as he asked us to?

Please, Saint Des, don't let it come to that.

Darryl and I have finished drinking, the icy water splashing numbingly into our empty stomachs, by the time Harry staggers up and thuds to his knees beside the stream. "Drink quickly, Harry," I tell him. "We gotta move."

"I" —*sip*— "hate" —*sip*— "you," he gasps.

"I know. Now, get up."

"I"—*gasp*—"can't."—*gasp*—"Gotta"—*gasp*—"rest!"

I grab him by his shirt shoulders and haul him upright, put my face very close to his. "Harry. Two choices. Run. Or die. Got it?"

HARRY

"We have to go faster, Harry," says Darryl gently. "You can do this. I know you can."

Josh's plain-speaking alone wouldn't have got me moving again. Or Darryl's encouragement. But, both together...somehow, I stiffen my legs under me as Josh releases my shirt. Somehow, I step forward at a run as they race off along the stream bank.

Somehow.

Run—or die.

Worse, run—or be left behind?

Josh's words come back to me, as he lay on that mountainside almost a year ago, weak and bleeding: *I'm bigger than you and you can't carry me. That's just a plain fact. If it gets to the point where I can't keep going, you leave me and get yourself back to the 'Vi. That's an order. Understand?*

If I can't keep going, what do I do? Beg them to stay here and die with me? How can I do that to them? Tell them to go, save themselves? Is that what Josh would expect me to do? I reckon so. Am I brave enough to do that? Die alone in the cold dark?

To save them? Or at least…to give them a chance?

An icy shiver runs down my back. No. No, that won't be necessary. I can keep up. I *can*.

Oh, Saint Des, help me keep up… Please?

JOSHUA

Only a trace of light remains as we reach the base of the mountain where the pass should be. Although I'm stumbling over rocks in the dark, I don't dare slacken my pace as I hurry up the bare open slopes above the treeline.

We *have* to find the path. Already, I can barely make out enough to navigate across this bleak expanse. Open ground and true night would bring even the most experienced hunter alive to a halt, without a good source of light.

I don't wait for Harry, just now. If I can find the path, I can call him to me. Making noise is a risk, sure, but not finding the path is worse. Contrary to what they show in movies, making fire, let alone gathering the right materials to construct enough torches to burn for several hours, is a very slow process. If we worked really fast, we might have finished making enough of them about when the storm killed us.

Ahead…boulders. I stare into the darkness, my

eyes straining wide as I try to catch as much light as I can, to *see…*

The shapes are familiar. I think I know where we are. I head left, as the boulders turn into an outcrop, then boulders again. And here…it's so dark I have to crouch and run my hands over the ground between the two crags, brushing a dusting of snow away and feeling…

Hard compacted ground underneath.

Footprints.

The path!

This pass, this path, isn't only used by humans, and it's well-trodden. Now we've found it, I can follow it right over the mountain and down the other side.

We made our first deadline. We beat the odds.

Now we just have to do it again.

DARRYL

Josh rises to his feet and leans against a boulder, breathing deeply in what I realize is relief more than exertion.

"Josh?"

"It's okay. I found the path. We made it in time."

"How are we going to follow it in the dark?" My voice comes out tense, no doubt betraying that I've been worrying about this. I can barely see now, but it's clear that there's open ground here and there on either side of the path. We could easily wander away from it.

Josh sighs. "I'm gonna have to take my boots off."

"What? It's freezing cold, Josh!" And getting colder by the hour as we gain altitude—and as the storm draws nearer.

"Mebbe not quite freezing yet, right here. Almost." Rustling clothing noises tell me that he's pulling his boots and socks off, tying the laces together and slinging the footwear around his neck—it's too dark to see him now. "We'll have to warm them as best we can now and then. No choice. We ain't got no light."

"Don't you have your fire steel?"

"No time, Darryl. Okay, here's Harry. Let's move."

JOSHUA

Rocks bruise my feet. Patches of cold, hard-packed snow chill and slice them. I push the pain to the back of my mind and plow on. Upwards. Upwards. Upwards. Toward the pass.

My hands reach out from side to side, tracing the boulders, the crags, the rock walls, the shale slopes we pass as my mind tries to keep me orientated on my mental map. When I do take a wrong turn and step off the path, my bare feet tell me at once as I crunch into loose snow or onto smooth trackless ground, and I can stop instantly and step back again. I'd *probably* feel if I stepped off with my boots on—but under the circumstances, *probably* just ain't good enough. If I lose this path, we all die.

We can't get ahead of Harry now, or he might take a wrong turn in the darkness. But whenever we have to stop to let Harry rest—too often—Darryl holds my feet to her warm stomach and puts her arms on top of them to warm them.

"I think your feet are bleeding, Josh," she says, one time.

"I know," is all I say. What can we do? The occasional patches of snow melt under my feet, damping them, mixing with the dust and dirt to coat the wounds in mud quick enough, masking the scent at least a little. Although, the snow is coming more often now, up here, and there's less dirt. Soon my feet are gonna be constantly snow-damp and bleeding freely. I'm gonna get frostbite if I can't get my boots back on soon.

Ain't nothing we can do.

It's totally dark, now, the type of darkness city-folk can't really conceive of. True night. No moon, no stars, no flame, no electric lights. Nothing. I can't see my hand in front of my face. Right now, my bare feet *are* our eyes. And without them, I'll be blind.

DARRYL

How much longer can Harry keep going? Exhaustion gnaws at me, and I'm much fitter than he is. How many hours of running remain? If it was nine hours until the storm arrives, and Josh thinks the timing is tight? Heck, will we have to run for another three, four hours or more?

Can I?

Can Harry? Why didn't I nag him more about his fitness, this last year? I guess I just didn't see enough of him, and he was so down anyway. And it didn't seem important.

Not important! Ha.

And Josh? How long can he keep going, with the abuse his feet are taking? Barefoot, up a mountain, in this weather? It must be freezing now. How long until his feet freeze as hard as the snow?

JOSHUA

My outstretched arms can finally touch rock walls on each side. We've reached what's normally the most perilous section—and the longest. From here, right up to the pass, and quite a way down the other side, the path is mostly narrow and confined. No space to go around any dangerous critter we might meet.

But also hard to get lost. And right now, the wind is coming from the side, meaning we're nicely sheltered from it.

Relief fills me as I warm my feet one last time on Darryl, then pull my socks on—thank God I kept them dry—then my boots. From the increasing numbness of my flesh, not a moment too soon, and frostbite's always further along than you think it is. I was beginning to think I were gonna have to choose between risking us all or risking losing toes or even my whole feet. But I don't have to expose my feet again for miles and miles and hours and hours, and thank God for that. If I do have to, it won't be good.

DARRYL

When we make it over the pass at last—we only know because Josh tells us, it's so dark now—Josh allows us a brief rest, finally. He settles us in the shelter of a boulder, shielded from the knifing wind which is suddenly cutting us now we've emerged from the pass. We can't even stare downslope at the terrain below to check for danger. It's invisible in the pitchy blackness.

"How do you even know the way?" I ask, when I've got my breath a little, sliding my ungloved hands under my top and against my stomach to warm them. I've been keeping them tucked under my armpits as much as possible, but they're still cold. Josh's feet were far colder; thank God he got his boots on again.

"Dad took me through every important pass on foot, one time or another," says Josh, as though that answers the question.

We haven't made a single terrain inspection since we stopped looking out for Seb, even though at first we had daylight. Every time I think about that fact, a feeling of naked vulnerability makes my skin crawl. We're breaking the rules into kindling, here.

But Josh is right. Our only options are to attempt to sit out a lightning-freeze, in the open, or throw caution to the wind and run thirty miles in the most reckless fashion imaginable.

No contest.

We get up again.

We run.

HARRY

I can't even see my feet, moving up and down in front of me. Up and down. Falling snow now flicks my face, my hands, settles damply on Josh's jacket, which I'm wearing right now, but I can't even see that. It's so cold.

If only we had a light.

My bad ankle, the one I sprained last Hallowtide, aches and wobbles under me more and more. My toes bump against rocks, rising ground, or over and over I almost fall—or do fall—as I find that the ground isn't where I expect it to be. At least up here on the mountainside there are few bushes to walk into. I'm covered in bruises already, but the fewer cuts the better—less blood scent to attract predators. Though some of the rocks cut me up pretty good when I land on them.

In a way, the worsening weather is a good thing. Soon, predators will be sensing the approaching lightning-freeze, and they'll be running for shelter with no thought for hunting.

At the moment...it's no worse than a bad flurry of snow.

I can't worry about carni'saurs, though. Can't think about anything but putting one blind, stumbling foot in front of the other. My body is so heavy.

"Might as well take these frights off," I mumble. "Nothing can see them, anyway..."

"Keep 'em on," comes Josh's relentless voice from in front of Darryl—though even he is panting hard, now. "Some critters see in the dark, y'know."

Including the Josh'osaurus? We *are* going slower now, as he gropes his way through the rocky landscape. But how is he even—

But I can't finish the thought. It's too hard work.

Run—or die alone, Harry.

Run.

JOSHUA

I plough on down the mountainside, my chest tight with exertion—but even more with fear that I might lose my way. If I do—even the too-slender chance we have is gone.

But I've been through this pass twice with Dad and once with Uncle Z. This was one they made sure to teach me well. 'Cause if you're lost in the area we've just come from, then—at least in summer—it's actually quicker and safer to cross this pass than to head the other way.

Unfortunately, it ain't summer, and there ain't no light at all.

No convenient moon, like in every movie I've ever seen.

And now…oh no, the rock walls are opening out again. I guess it's good, really, 'cause it means we're getting well down the mountain, but it also means the chances of losing the path are rising. But my feet are aching, pins and needles stabbing me sharply. I've got frostbite already. If I take my boots off, it'll make it far worse, and in next to no time I won't be able to feel the path anyway—so it ain't worth risking crippling my-self. I'm just gonna have do my best to sense the terrain through my boots.

I try to drive all thoughts out of my head and let instinct take over, try to stop straining my eyes uselessly and let my hands feel the shape of the rocks. Let my throbbing feet feel the worn stone, the hard-packed snow...

We're still on the path. My feet tell me that, even if my eyes are next-to useless.

On. Faster. On. On. On...

HARRY

My legs shake under me like jello. How much longer can I go on? I don't know what's around me—could be boulders, open ground, forest, hungry T. rex—and I'm too tired to care. I stumble on after Darryl

And on.

And on...

Terrible screeches split the night, feet away, sending a feeble rush of adrenaline through me.

Raptors? My weary mind grinds painfully slowly.

Uh-oh...*Dakotaraptors*?

Man-sized...

Have we blundered into a pack?

We are *dead*.

A full-volume T. rex roar, from just in front me, actually jolts a larger bolt of adrenaline through my exhausted body, before I realize that it's probably Josh.

No way to be sure, in this darkness.

JOSHUA

Roaring as loudly as I can, I jab my spear at where my ears tell me the closest Dakotaraptor is. The point connects with something—I try to drive the spear further in, roaring even louder.

The raptor screeches in pain as it recoils from the spear, making my ears ring.

I stumble after it, lunging again, lunging and roaring as if I'm not afraid of them and mean to kill and eat them all. All or nothing. If they don't run, we're dead.

Beside me, the sound of wood scraping rock, another pained screech, and a splintering noise suggest that Darryl is lunging blindly at them as well.

A sound to my right...claws tapping... I spin and stab, roaring hoarsely.

Another screech—the spear is yanked from my clutching hands—and finally, the blessed sound of claws pattering away over rock. Many claws.

They're leaving.

HARRY

"Keep going," I hear Josh murmur to Darryl, then Darryl's hand grabs hold of mine, pulling me forward at a dead-run, despite the darkness and the stony ground. Is she holding onto Josh?

The scuffing-tapping sounds have already receded into the sound of the rising wind, which is beginning to make an eerie hum through the rocks. Every time we pause, Darryl cups her hands over my nose and ears, trying to keep them warm. Or, at least, unfrozen. I try to do the same for her or Josh, but they keep telling me to get my hands back under my armpits at once.

"I broke my spear," mutters Darryl, maybe to Josh, maybe to herself.

"Darn raptor ran off with mine," Josh mutters back. "Don't think I stuck it in that hard, it just snagged in its feathers."

My spear snapped…I don't know how long ago. It wasn't cut out to be a walking stick.

We stagger on. And on…

Did we really just fight off a pack of Dakotaraptors?

I guess with the approaching storm, dinner may not be their priority right now. I wouldn't have thought the weather counted as that bad, yet, though.

Maybe we just got lucky. Didn't Josh say that his Uncle Z once—

I lose the thread of my thought.

And stagger blindly on.

Run—or die alone.

DARRYL

I can't believe we got out of that in one piece. I guess we were just too unfamiliar prey, out here in the wild.

We fought too hard, so they played it safe and cleared off. Although predators need more food in the cold winter months, hunting is often easier, too. Prey animals weakened by the harsh conditions make easy pickings. They didn't need to bother with us.

Right?

On the other hand, winter's barely started. This unexpected lightning-freeze is shockingly early. But they do seem to have gone. Good thing, since we're now unarmed.

How much did we actually scare them? Josh tows us on more ruthlessly than ever. Wanting to put distance between us and the pack?

Good plan.

HARRY

Darryl keeps hold of me, dragging me after her. We're going faster than before. How long can I stay on my feet?

Or...I stumble over a boulder and crash to my knees again...how long can I keep getting up?

Panting, her arms trembling with tiredness, Darryl is already hauling me up again. I lean against her, frantic for support, and she sways slightly—but then pulls my arm over her shoulders. We move forward together, but my weight makes her pant even harder, her breath going thready.

Soon enough, hands close around my other arm, pulling it across a broader set of shoulders. Josh.

We stagger onwards like a six-legged drunk, but all too soon the path starts threading between narrow rocks again. Suddenly, we're shielded from the wind again—that feels good—and slightly refreshed after their support, I can walk by myself. I have to.

Until my bad foot turns under me on a loose rock, and I go down—hearing and feeling the ominous lightning-agony *crack* as my ankle bone snaps.

JOSHUA

Harry yells in pain until I reach him in a couple of groping steps and clap my palm over his mouth. "Quiet! Don't sound so darn tasty!" When I think he's got himself under control, I ease my hand away. "What happened?"

"I fell." There's a tight-held-back sob in his voice, but he don't scream again. "My ankle...it...it broke."

I suck in a breath, dismayed. My elbow is against Darryl's side, and I feel her do the same. I grope for his foot with my numb, clumsy fingers, checking—Harry smothers a groan.

"Yeah, I think it's broken," I confirm. "*Misfire. Misfire-misfire-misfire.*"

Belatedly, I think: *Sorry, Saint Des. But I guess you know how I feel.*

Guess I don't need to agonize no more about what to do about Harry. Fortunately, it's an easy decision now.

HARRY

"Okay, let's find a crack, quickly," says Josh to Darryl. "Anything he can get inside for warmth and protection. And bushes, for scent-cam."

"We *will* be able to—"

Josh cuts her off impatiently. "Yes, we're far enough down the mountain now, we can bring the 'Vi up here as soon as we get it back, and pick him up. A crack, quickly!"

A terrible clenching starts in my guts, works up to my stomach, seizes my heart, my throat.

Don't leave me! That's what's lodged in my throat.

Don't leave me! If I say that to Darryl, won't she stay?

Darryl doesn't reply to Josh at all. Doesn't say that she'll stay with me, that Josh should go on. Of course she doesn't. Josh might not even make it to the 'Vi alone, if he took a tumble and hurt himself, or fell prey to some predator that might've run from two humans. And even if he did, he'd be tackling Seb all by himself, instead of with Darryl—which would cut our chances in half that one of them would come away alive and in control of the 'Vi.

But as I listen to my sister groping around in the darkness, searching for somewhere to stash me, while Josh does the same, the rational thoughts fly apart like the snow whirling in the wind. They're going to leave me. They're going to run off into the darkness and leave me to die in the storm. Alone...

"Here." Josh calls in a low voice. "Let's get him into it."

They take my arms, haul me up, drag me between them. I'm too numb with pain and fear and exhaustion to help them—or fight them. When we finally stop, Darryl hugs me tightly and finally speaks.

"I love you, Harry. We'll be back real soon, okay?"

If you're so sure you'll be back real soon, why did you say the first thing?

I hug her back, hard—saying nothing.

Josh gives me a quick hug. "Sit tight, Harry," he says briskly—like I can do anything else with a broken ankle. "We'll be back in about...three, four, five hours, tops."

I don't know what time it is, but I have a feeling that's cutting it awfully close with the storm.

Josh checks the zipper on his coat, which I've been wearing for—for far more than my share of the time, now that I think about it—and then...

Oh no! *Ouch.* They're rolling me and shoving me into a deep crack under a—I can't see what. Can't see them, can't see anything, not since darkness fell. Could be a massive cliff or a small boulder for all I know.

I keep my mouth shut and let them. I keep my mouth shut because if I open it, I'm gonna beg them to stay.

And then they're going to die too.

DARRYL

"Quick," says Josh. "Pile some branches across the crack. Then we heap snow over it, as much as we can. But quickly! We gotta get to the 'Vi even faster now."

And we've been going too slow as it is... I can almost hear him finishing the sentence in his head.

We break branches from a bush that doesn't want to yield them to us with fingers already stinging and burning from hours of exposure and rough rock, drag them for what feels like far too far, and pile them over Harry's hide-out.

Am I really going to do this? Leave my little brother here?

But how else can I save him? If we stay, he definitely dies. If we leave...he might live. I guess I'm more likely to live than he is, since I'll get into the 'Vi faster — guilt fills my stomach, nipping at my insides like a shoal of piranha'saurs. Then again, Harry won't be tackling Seb bare-handed.

"Now the snow," orders Josh, though I'm sure

he'd normally insist we cut vastly more scent-cam.

But, right now, speed is more important than anything.

HARRY

My chill fingers touch branches...and snow. Soft coldness covers the crack all the way across now. I'm sealed in.

No... A branch pokes me in the ribs as someone jiggles it, and Josh's voice comes, slightly muffled.

"Give this stick a wiggle every few minutes, Harry. It's keeping your air hole clear. But the snow's gonna keep you warm, okay? And keep that coat on. Even if you feel like you don't need it, you *keep it on*. Just sit tight. We'll have the 'Vi back up here as quick as we can."

"Bye, Harry," comes Darryl's voice, bright with fake-cheer. "See you soon."

Guess I probably will see them soon. But we'll all be on the carpet before the Almighty, like as not.

"Okay, Harry?" comes Josh's voice again.

They're about to leave.

Last chance to beg them to stay.

Last chance to say...anything.

I fight with my own voice box as my mouth opens.

Or maybe with my own self. A vicious knock-down, drag-out, wrestling match. Finally, a thin squeak emerges from my throat, aimed toward that little air hole.

DARRYL

"It's okay. Go." I just catch Harry's words, whispering through that small breathing passage. And then, "Love you both."

Almost, I break. Almost, I start digging through that snow, pulling the branches aside, to take my little brother in my arms, to promise him I'll never leave him...

But Josh grips my hand, pulling me to my feet. My heart can't save Harry. Only my head.

My heart hurting far more than my hands or my legs, I follow Josh into the darkness.

JOSHUA

Now that we're not waiting for Harry every few strides, we're making better time. My heart lifts slightly. Mebbe we'll make it. It can't be far to the stopping place, now.

The flurrying snow has eased temporarily, and the

wind with it, thank God. A distant flash of lightning within the storm system—the first light we've seen for hours—gives a brief, sudden, disorientating restoration of sight, over almost before we can register it. It probably ain't done our night vision no good, but without any light, that don't even matter. But I saw the lightning reflect dimly off the lake, there at the bottom of this mountain.

The 'Vi should be down there. Seb were driving like the devil to get over that pass before the storm blocked it. He had a good head start. He should be there already.

He'd better be. We left the coat with Harry. Even in my boots, my feet feel increasingly numb, never properly warm after being exposed earlier. Walking on them is the wrong thing to do, but I ain't got no choice. I can barely feel the trail.

But we ain't lost, yet.

So long as the 'Vi is there, we can still make it. We can still save Harry.

I glance uneasily into the darkness, to the north. The snow will be back soon, with a vengeance, and the wind, too, but right now…more lightning flashes in the distance. The brief, faint glimpses of the terrain ahead are useful, but…

Heck, the storm is close now. Can we really get back to Harry in time?

DARRYL

I stumble on after Josh, grateful for the regular lightning that finally gives me back some vision. And for the real hope burning in my breast. Because Josh *does* think we have a chance. There is no way he'd have left Harry, otherwise. He'd have stayed so we could at least all die together.

"How," I gasp, as I run, "do we take back the 'Vi, Josh?"

"Thinking about it," he pants. "Depends if Seb is awake or asleep."

"Be asleep...won't he?" I wheeze.

"Mebbe. Mebbe still getting everything locked down for the storm." Josh stumbles wearily over a boulder with an unusual clumsiness that betrays how exhausted he is and maybe how numb or sore his feet are. "Mebbe taking a nap first. Depends how fast he got over that mountain."

"Josh," I'm panting almost too hard to speak, but I've gotta say this, "you know I can't find Harry again, in this, right? So if only one of us makes it out with the 'Vi, it's gotta be you. Tell me you understand that."

He hurries on in silence for so long I think he's not gonna answer. But finally:

"Yeah." Never have I heard him speak a word with more reluctance, but he says it. "But let's make sure we *both* make it out, okay?"

I guess this conversation is pointless. Bending over

backward to try to keep Josh—who's by far the stronger of the two of us—out of harm's way will just make us more likely to fail. What happens will happen.

We hurry on without speaking. However much I want to plan, save every second I can, talking's too hard.

Neither of us discuss what we'll do if the 'Vi isn't there. It's not like we'd dare head back up the mountain to Harry, in case the 'Vi turned up after we left.

And it doesn't exactly take much forward planning to freeze to death.

JOSHUA

Almost down to the valley floor. This is the stopping place, at last. But where's the 'Vi? It should be right here.

I slow down, scanning the darkness, waiting for the lightning.

Where are you, Seb?

Several flashes later, we're still jogging—stumbling—through the area, fear clenching my chest tighter and tighter, like a rex's jaws are closing around me. And this time, I don't have no electric prod in its mouth to drive it off.

No sign of it in any of the best places.

Seb, where—?

A tiny glint of metal, close to the rocks—the rex releases my chest.

"There," I breathe to Darryl. I grab her hand and pull her down behind a good solid boulder. We peep over it, waiting—*flash*—waiting—*flash*...

"No lights," I whisper, once I'm sure. "Shutters are all closed. Hopefully he's asleep. It's safe to try to get in, then."

Or as safe as it can be...

"What do we do then? Don't we need a plan?

"A new spear would be a good idea," I concede. "Let's get a couple, real quick, and make our move."

No time to waste. Harry could be dead from hypothermia before the storm even reaches him, the state he were in. Though I ain't gonna say that to Darryl.

From the speed with which she looks around for branches, I don't need to.

DARRYL

"There might be a bush over there," I tell Josh.

"Too small. We're gonna have to go a little further down. I see trees."

Silently, I curse the extra time that will take—yet taking on Seb bare-handed is setting ourselves up to fail. Josh rises to his feet. I rise too...only to stumble into him as he goes rigid and motionless ahead of me.

I know better than to speak when he's standing like that.

Listening.

He grabs my hand, towing me after him as he races flat-out toward the 'Vi.

My legs shake and wobble under me. This kind of speed is almost more than they can give me, after the night we've had.

I stagger against Josh as he halts by the rear of the vehicle, almost falling—his hands grip my arms, holding me up until my legs steady again.

"We're going straight in?" I breathe.

"The pack followed us," he whispers back.

My breath catches, and I swing around, my eyes stabbing uselessly at the blackness.

How close are they? Guess they decided we weren't that scary, after all.

Close enough that Josh caught a sound over the wind...or did he glimpse a feathery tail in a lightning flash?

Josh is busy with the control pad that unlocks the tiny manual hatch providing access into the rear pen. Clever Josh. No motors, no pneumatics to make whirrs or hisses and wake Seb.

I barely catch the tiny snick as the lock unfastens. Then Josh is lifting the hatch with painstaking care.

Yeah, the tiniest clank could kill us...

Another flash...he's holding the hatch up with one

hand...his other hand grips the waistband of my pants at the back, boosting me up...I slide my shoulders through the gap...and I'm in. I crouch immediately and slip my hand through, fighting to hold the hatch up so he can get in himself without making noise. The hatch, which weighs nothing, normally, is a crushing weight on my shaking arm. But Josh is up and in, taking it from me, easing it gently, gently, gently down.

Snick.

We're safe from the raptors.

But the worst danger may be in here with us.

JOSHUA

Darryl quivers with tension beside me. To escape the pack, we've jumped back into Seb's frying pan—unarmed. And now, unlike earlier, there are only two of us. Our chances of overpowering him are worse, rather than better.

Well...no. Not when he's probably asleep, and thinks we're thirty miles away, shivering and crying and waiting to freeze to death. Part of me still can't believe he saw that storm coming and just drove off with the 'Vi, left us. Even though I know full-well he were gonna shoot us himself.

How do we take him down? If we wait, he's gonna come back here eventually and find us—and we'll die.

And we can't wait, anyways. If we do—Harry will

die. And we can't even survive the storm here in the rear pen, with no warm clothes and sleeping bags and heating.

We have to take Seb out—right now.

DARRYL

"Gun cabinet?" I breathe in Josh's ear.

Josh moves to the control panel by the door from the pen into the main living area, lifting the protective cover that prevents stock from damaging it, and swipes at it, checking the internal cameras.

"Seb's in the cab bedroom," he breathes, also right in my ear. "Better chance to get the guns without him hearing if he were in the overCab."

"What choice do we have?"

"Yeah." Without another word, he carefully slides open the manual door from the rear pen into the living area. I follow him through. But our reaching hands touch an open gun cabinet door—inside, it's empty.

Without a word to each other, we retreat back into the rear pen.

"He's got them all in the cab," Josh breathes. "Mebbe he looked on the map. Or mebbe he just wants them all available if the police catch up with him. We ain't getting them anyways."

Coldness shivers through every vein, and it's not just from running for hours through icy temperatures without enough clothes on. What are we gonna do? Just sit back here and wait for Seb to find us while Harry dies? Lure him out and try to club him with a folding chair? Could we get the shovel out of the cupboard without making too much noise?

Josh bends over the little control screen again and starts swiping through the external cameras, so I stay quiet. After a second, he taps a finger to the small screen, pointing. I look closer, and a shiver goes down my spine.

A full-grown female Dakotaraptor is peering straight into the side entrance's door-cam. We got inside not a moment too soon. Josh selects another camera, and there's the rest of the pack, sniffing around that side of the 'Vi.

Josh stares at the screen for a moment. "Okay," he whispers, "stay here."

With that, he slides through into the living area again. What the—?

Only moments later, he's back, sliding the door closed again and locking it carefully.

An ominous coppery scent fills the air...blood.

In fact, he's holding his left arm well away from him in a weird way, the other hand holding the kitchen drying cloth clamped against it. I draw the cloth away and in the dim light of the screen, I glimpse...

Toothmarks. Human. He's bitten his own arm savagely.

"What the—?"

"Needed plenty of blood." He grits his teeth for a moment, clearly suppressing a wince. "Can't worry about that now. The pack won't stay around long, not with that storm on the way."

Needed plenty of blood...the pack...suddenly, I think I know where this is going.

"We need him to dash through right away," Josh breathes in my ear, as I quickly knot the cloth around his arm to make it stay, "with no time to stop and think or look out the window, okay? We speak through the observation slit, so it sounds like we're out there by the gun cabinet."

I swallow. Swallow my protests, as he touches the control panel again. The side door hisses noisily back, letting in the snow, the wind—and the pack. Despite the temperature, sweat breaks out all over me. Seb has to have heard that. This fence has gone live—we're committed.

Silence from the cab, though.

The 'Vi shifts as the first curious she-raptor leaps up into the opening, dipping her head to sniff eagerly around the cab doorway. At the blood splashed there?

"Get the guns!" Josh speaks in a low voice, but loud enough to be heard from the cab, like someone over-excited who thinks he's being quieter than he's actually being.

"They're all gone!" I put in, making myself sound

panicked—not hard, with my heart pounding harder than hard. Heck, if this doesn't work... "Grab the shovel, quick!"

"Wilson!" The furious bellow comes from the cab, and the sound of feet thudding to the floor. "How the *he*—"

The raptor screeches loudly in response to the unfamiliar sounds.

"There's a raptor out here, Seb," shouts Josh urgently. "Don't come out!"

"You take me for a fool?" sneers Seb from the cab, as something clanks against the wall just the other side of the cab door—probably his rifle tip. "I'm gonna put a bullet in your belly and make you *watch* while I—"

The cab door hisses open.

Seb screams.

The rifle fires.

Then clatters to the floor.

For terrible, long moments, Seb's shrieks mix with the raptor's triumphant snarls—then both give way to horrible, wet, tearing noises.

Josh holds me tightly, so tightly, with his blood-free arm, keeping my face turned away from the hatch, as we stay utterly motionless, utterly silent. But he's looking, I know he is. Watching through that observation hatch. Watching until he's quite sure the threat is gone.

One threat.

We go on standing absolutely still and silent. The rear pen isn't designed to contain anything as large as a wide-awake and un-tranquilized Dakotaraptor. And although Josh is being very careful not to get the blood on me, he stinks of it. We aren't safe.

I feel the 'Vi shift twice as two more raptors spring inside.

But soon, thank God, come the sounds of something being dragged outside as more snarling, hissing raptors grab for it. The 'Vi shifts, once, twice, thrice, as the raptors follow. And then the sounds of raptor feasting suddenly dim as Josh taps the control panel and the side door slides closed. And locks.

We're alone in the 'Vi.

We're safe.

But Harry is still out there.

And Seb...

Seb is dead, and I don't know how I feel about that.

Other than safer.

Much, much safer.

HARRY

I have never been so cold in my life. My teeth rap jarringly against each other as my body shakes convulsively, on and on. I press my hands deeper into my armpits, desperately seeking warmth, but they won't go any further in. I can barely feel my feet, though I fight to keep wiggling my toes, the way Josh taught me to do in a situation like this.

Josh. Who left me.

He and Darryl both left me.

To save you, Harry...

But I can barely hear the dim whisper anymore. My thoughts are so slow and heavy.

All I know is that I'm alone.

Am I? I guess God is here. And maybe Saint Des and the other saints and Mom are hovering around me.

It's not the same as having my big sis here to wrap me in her arms and tell me everything will be okay.

So, so cold...

But I guess I should make the best of what company I have. Twitching my fingertips in my armpits to keep track, I begin a chaplet of Saint Desmond.

Jesus, I trust in you.

Jesus, I trust in you.

Jesus, I trust in you...

Do I? I trust that He'll forgive me for all the times I messed up or was mean when I could have been nicer, done better, since I'm sorry. But do I trust he's going to get me out of this?

I guess I believe that He *could*.

Whether He will? How can I know that?

Jesus, I trust in you.

Jesus, I trust in you.

Jesus, I trust in you...

I've lost count. Never mind. *Just start again, Harry.*

At least my teeth aren't chattering anymore. Maybe the snow's insulating my little crack better than I expected.

Oh yeah, I need to... I grope for my stick and wiggle it. A blast of chill, fresh air hits my face harder than ever. Is the wind rising out there?

I try to pray again, but soon lose track. I'm so warm now, I've completely stopped shivering.

Maybe I should take off this jacket. I've got a vague feeling that I shouldn't, but why? Clearly I don't need it anymore…

DARRYL

For several more long moments, we cling so tightly to one another that I can feel Josh's heart beating against my chest, far too fast. Can he feel mine?

Finally, still taking great care to keep his bleeding arm away, Josh eases free of me.

"Please, just...just wait here for a moment." His voice comes strangled in the dimness. "Just wait here. Please?"

A click as he unlocks the sliding door, and he's limping through into the living area. A clang as he closes the observation hatch, blocking my view, then light floods through the open door.

I stand silently, until the scraping, sloshing sounds finally penetrate my numb brain.

He's cleaning up.

Part of me wants to stay right here until he's done it.

But...that's not fair. He didn't lure Seb out of that cab by himself. Why should only he have to get Seb's blood on his hands?

It takes me a moment to overcome my reluctance, then I manage to take those few steps through that door. I'm afraid to look, but...there's not much to see. Josh crouches near the cab doorway, now wiping the floor with a gloved hand full of odorControl wipes. A few crimson splashes dot the doorway and the walls, but he's got the worst of it up already.

"Josh? Can I help?"

He glances around, and I can tell he's sorry I've come out before he's finished, but...well, it's really not that bad, now. So he just says, "Yeah, grab some gloves and wipes and get any obvious blood. We can deep-clean after the storm. We gotta get to Harry."

"Should we even be doing *this* now?" Every moment Harry's out there...

"If we don't," he says grimly, "blood will get track-ed all over the 'Vi. And we can't risk that. And when I say deep-clean later, we gotta get it all, Darryl. Every last speck."

"D'you reckon Seb smells tastier than other folks?"

I can't help saying, though I've already started running the wipes around as quickly as I can.

"It ain't the carni'saurs I'm worried about." Josh carries on wiping frantically as he speaks. "It's the cops and the elders. I just took a super-quick look on the console, and I think Seb wiped the camera footage. If he did…then no one can know about this. No one. Ever."

A mini blizzard blows through my stomach. Is he saying—? My voice goes almost…shrill. "It was self-defense, Josh! He was trying to kill us!"

"Yeah, he were. I ain't saying we done nothing wrong, Darryl, okay? But without those videos, how do we prove it? Three to one, *we* coulda just as easily driven him out here to murder *him*."

I swipe the wipes over the front cupboards. "For what motive?"

"Mebbe we found out what he did to your dad. Mebbe I wanted to benefit from that share Wilhelm left me. Mebbe I just hated his guts. Too many motives. We clean, and we tell no one. Not even Harry."

"He's going to guess…"

"He can guess until Triceratops hatching time, we don't tell him, and we forbid him to talk about this whole trip out-city, okay? Safer for him, and safer for us."

Safer for him? Is Josh afraid that Harry could get blamed for this too? The city-folk would put him in juvie and the elders...well, I don't even know what the Hunter elders would do, if they decided he counted as a man. A man who had murdered someone.

"We tell no one," I agree, swiping at one last smear of blood. "Come on, I think that's all of it."

Josh crouches unsteadily, turning slowly, scanning everywhere. A couple of times his hand flashes out, catching some missed speck. Then he rises to his feet and circles the living area, doing the same thing. An instant dressing covers the wound on his left arm—guess he slapped that on at once to avoid adding to the mess.

"Okay," Josh agrees, completing his inspection and rolling his sleeves down again. "That'll do for now. Let's get Harry."

JOSHUA

Snow clogs the wipers as I turn back into the wind for the next zag up the mountainside. The visibility is horrendous, and I have to drop to a crawl. Impatience heats my belly, but I ain't got no choice. If I drive us off a cliff, or break an axle, there'll be no chance of getting to Harry at all.

I glance at the radar map, since we're inside the leading edge of the storm now, and too close to see it with our eyes—not as a whole, anyway.

Heck, the eye is getting close. If Harry's still alive,

he won't be when that hits. Even Darryl and I won't be, if we ain't tucked up warm to wait for it to go over.

But not yet. We've got a little more time.

My feet ache and burn, prickling fiercely as I press the pedals, but I welcome the pain. Pain means they ain't frozen through. I got my boots back on in time.

Dimly, I make out a gap in the boulders. Time to turn again. That takes us out of the wind, and visibility improves fractionally as the snow stops piling onto the windshield. It still fills the air, thick and heavy, blocking most of the view. If I drive us into a dead end...

Ain't nothing I can do but keep going and hope I ain't lost. From the occasional glimpses of boulders, each with their distinctive shapes and formations, I don't think I am. But we sure ain't got time to be lost.

Harry ain't got time.

DARRYL

Josh eases us to a halt. For a moment I think he's looking which way to go next, then he applies the parking brake and cuts the engine, sliding out of the driver's seat and moving to the side door. "Come on. This is as close as we can get."

He grabs his snow pants, which I laid out ready while we drove, pulls them on over his tattered cotton, then picks up the backpack containing Harry's snow gear, which I've also packed. He secures a blizzard tether and belt over his jacket, then pulls on his full winter hat, snow goggles and gloves. I'm already muffled up ready in mine.

"Got the rope?" he asks, speaking loudly to be heard over the storm.

"Here." I snap a karabiner to his belt. On the end of about five feet of rope, the other karabiner is already hooked to my own belt, beside my tether reel.

"Harry's too far away for us both to use tethers," Josh tells me. "We'll have to join them together and hope they reach. So don't unhook from me for any reason. You got that extra line?"

"In the backpack." If we run out of the tidy, self-retracting tether cord, we'll have to use a spool of standard paracord, and it'll be much slower.

"Okay, let's get Harry." He opens the side door, letting in the howling blizzard, and leaps down.

There's no point one of us trying to provide cover, with visibility as it is and Harry so far away. And it will take both of us to get Harry back here, in our exhausted condition. I follow him without a word. He doesn't pick up his rifle, so I don't, either. Guess nothing matters right now except speed, and carting a large chunk of metal along will only slow us down.

What's going to be out hunting in this, anyway? Anything with a scrap of brains—or instinct—will be hunkering down in the best possible shelter by now.

I lower myself from the 'Vi, stiff and aching from all that running, while Josh fastens his tether to the external belay point and double-checks it's secure, then I follow him into the snow. At least we're suited up in our winter gear, now, and holding powerful flashlights.

After only a few steps, we're engulfed in whirling whiteness that reflects the electric light back at us dazzlingly. Josh drops his flashlight to a lower setting and the glare grows less, visibility fractionally better, so I do the same. Then, flashlights or not, rope or not, he grabs tight hold of my hand and draws me after him.

Outage, can even Josh find his way back to Harry, in this? Then again, he just led us over that pass in complete darkness.

Saint Des, pray for us. Lord, guide him...

JOSHUA

I've always been real good at finding my way, but this is insane.

"Thank you, Dad," I whisper, the words whipped from my numb lips almost before I know they were there. "Thank you, Uncle Z."

They gave me some real unpleasant blizzard navigation training, as well as tether training, when I were little. And not so little. They'd drop me off, then drive a short way and wait for me to find my way back to the 'Vi. I mean, they had me in sight on the heat scanners, the whole time. I knew I weren't in no real danger. But being lost in the cold is a particular kind of scary. Far too easy to panic, and panic kills you. But thanks to them, I ain't gonna panic. Even if I can barely see any more than I could in the darkness. We're tethered. We're fine. It's Harry who's in danger, if I can't find him.

I push the thoughts away, push all thoughts away. I *can* find Harry. But the moment I start thinking too hard, I'm gonna start second guessing myself. I've just gotta *go* to him.

One hand resting on the unspooling tether line, checking, just constantly checking it's still there, and keeping tight hold of Darryl, I hurry through the snow, floundering through the gathering drifts, peering through the whirling flakes at anything distinctive.

We should be almost to the footpath...

Do I know that rock? I kneel and shove snow away...hard-beaten ground beneath. Yes. We've found the path.

"Come on!" I move forward, but a yank at my belt, a twang of cord against my gloved fingertips jerks me to a halt. "We're out of tether. Let's hook yours up!"

I pull my gloves off, cold or no cold. It's too fiddly a job, and if the fully-extended tether jerks from my hands and flies away into the snow, we'll never find it again. There's a reason why you're never *ever* supposed to unclip the thing from your belt while outside. But, then, what idiot would ever go more than 660 feet from their 'Vi in a blizzard and need to?

There! My tether is now attached to Darryl's. We're safe. I try to let out a sigh of relief, but a vicious icy gust snatches it from me, sucking all the air from my lungs. Coughing, I tug on Darryl's hand as I choke, "Come on…"

I'm not sure if she hears me over the wind, but she hurries to keep up as I draw her on again, up, up, ever up the mountain. My sore, burning, prickling feet sear as my boots rub them. Should not be walking on them. Nope.

Too bad.

Where's Harry? We're gonna run out of the second tether soon. If we have to start messing around with the paracord, it's gonna take so long.

Yeah, we're gonna run out of tether any moment now. My gut tells me, loud and clear. "We're getting to the end of the line," I yell to Darryl. "Go carefully."

Last thing we need is for a jerk to separate it from the first tether or yank it from her belt somehow.

We move forward more cautiously, but then…

"I think we're here!" I rush to a boulder and run my hands over it. Is it the right one? I never saw it, earlier, not with my eyes. If I'm wrong…

I think I'm right. I prop the flashlight on the

boulder and start digging frantically in the heaped up drifts with my gloved hands. But there's nothing but snow. Am I wrong? We don't have time for me to be wrong!

"Yes!" Darryl's cry just reaches me, and I glance around to see her hauling out a broken-off branch, tumbling a heap of snow away. I *am* right. There's just more snow collected on top than I expected.

I dig harder than ever. Soon my gloved fingers close around a branch. I haul backward, trying to use the foliage to pull as much snow away as possible, then reach into the crack, searching.

Has he suffocated, in there? Frozen to death?

My gloved fingers touch something soft. Flesh? I grip a limb and pull. Part-way out, Darryl gets a grip as well, and suddenly Harry's sliding out twice as fast. He's taken the coat off, curse it. Musta got hypothermic. His head flops limply—he's un-conscious, if nothing worse.

From the far distance, a gust of wind brings an ominous *crack, crack, crackle* sound to my ears. Fear floods me. We're a quarter-mile from the 'Vi!

"Let's get his winter coat on him, quick," I shout to Darryl.

"Is he alive?" Darryl screams the words, partly to be heard over the storm and partly...well, I know how she feels.

"We ain't got time to find out. Just get it on him

and let's go!"

I turn him so she can put it around him, his arms tucked inside with him for the sake of his hands, zip it up, draw the hood tightly up over his head. Then I chuck him over my shoulder and lift. I thought I would need Darryl's help to carry him, but the adrenaline is back. We're almost out of time.

"Just lead the way!" I shout to Darryl. "And *run*! I ain't joking!"

DARRYL

Somehow, Josh is carrying Harry all by himself. I know he's strong and tough, but I can hardly believe it. He was staggering almost as much as me on the way up here on his cut-up, frostbitten feet. Now, he plows after me as though he's possessed, urging me on if I slacken the pace even a little.

Crack-crackle-crack...

That noise is getting louder. The noise I first heard just before Josh picked Harry up and took off. Suddenly, I realize what it is; why it got Josh moving so frantically.

Not that far away, at least in meteorological terms, water, earth, plants, trees, everything, is freezing solid as the eye of the storm reaches it. And when it reaches us puny humans, we'll freeze too.

Energy zips into my own leaden legs, propelling

me forward. Suddenly I'm clutching at the tether as I try to follow it almost faster than it can spool.

We have to reach the 'Vi! Now!

JOSHUA

We're running—shambling, staggering—running back down the mountainside. The rope is taut between us, since I need both hands to keep Harry aboard. Darryl's flashlight weaves a crazy pattern all over the ground ahead 'cause she's clipped it to her shoulder to leave both her hands free for the tether, which she's following with desperate speed. Snow hammers my goggles in a constant frozen assault as I peer through the blizzard in an attempt to see the ground in front of my unhappy feet, to see obstacles before I fall— agonizingly—over them.

The rope suddenly yanks me to the right, almost sending me toppling into a snowdrift. We've reached the turn-off!

Thank you, Saint Des, thank you, Lord.

I stumble on behind Darryl, Harry an ominous deadweight crushing me downwards from shoulders to screaming feet as I run. Not far now.

Please, not far.

Is Harry alive? Stopping to check would only have made him colder, but if he's gone, carrying him is just reducing our own chances. But with our hands so cold, and him so cold, how could we even be sure? We've just gotta get him to the 'Vi.

Please be alive, Harry. Please?

DARRYL

Where's the 'Vi? The wind brings the *crack-crackle* to us more and more often, louder and louder. Every breath burns my throat and lungs, the air is so cold now. And it's about to get much colder.

After all this, after everything, are we going to die out here? We must be so close...

Lord, help us!

Nothing.

I can feel Josh flagging behind me, the rope jerking more and more as he stumbles and almost falls and drags himself on…

Nothing.

It's so cold… I *have* to get them to the 'Vi!

Still the tether spools itself.

Something reflects ahead of us. Is it...?

Metal!

JOSHUA

I heave Harry off my shoulder, sliding him into the 'Vi, then climb in after, turning to help Darryl up. She unhooks the tether reel from her belt with fumbling fingers and tosses it outside, allowing the door to hiss closed, shutting out the blizzard. Only now do I realize how hard I'm shivering despite all my snow gear. No time to worry about it now.

I roll Harry over, pulling the hood back from his face. Frost thickens his eyebrows, his eyelashes, lays over his cheeks. His lips are blue. I pull off my glove and put my chilled fingers to his neck, searching for a pulse.

"I think...I think he's alive," I tell Darryl, as she stares at me, unbreathing. The pulse is faint, but I don't think I'm imagining it. I hope to God I ain't. "Let's get him warm. We've gotta hunker down too. Eye will be here any minute."

She helps me lift him up into the overCab bedroom, the warmest space in the vehicle.

"Zip two sleeping bags together, double-layered," I tell her quickly. "Get him inside, get your outer layers off and get in there with him."

I grope in the first aid cupboard and shove a handful of frostbite packs into her hand, three pairs of the glove ones and three pairs of foot ones as well as some for ears and cheeks and noses. "Put these on his fingers, toes, nose, ears. Anywhere that might be frozen. They won't warm him, of course, but they'll reduce the damage." I grab a handful of standard heat packs and give them to her as well. "And these heat ones on his torso, to help bring his temperature up."

"Aren't you coming?" But she chucks her handful up into the doorway and begins to climb up right away.

"As soon as I have the 'Vi ready for the storm. Coupla things I gotta do."

Hobbling to the kitchen area, I quickly fill two thermos flasks with hot water from the boiler tap—just two, no time for more—then hit the buttons to jettison all our liquids. Freshwater, gray water, everything. I hope the pipes ain't already froze, but it's too late to worry about it. Then I set the heater to the storm setting, so it will prioritize keeping the overCab bedroom warm above all else.

Did Technicolor service the heater when they were getting the 'Vi ready for my release? I sure hope so. But I'd never normally in a million years put myself in the path of a killer-chiller with a heater I ain't serviced myself for more than twelve months. Especially stuck up on a mountain in a darn stupid position like this.

Too late now. We're inside the 'Vi, and that's as good as we can manage.

I shove the thermoses up into the berth and climb up after them, closing the door carefully.

"You got those packs on him?" I ask Darryl, pulling off my wet jacket and chucking it to the far end of the berth so it can't get us wet. I have to shout over the noise of the howling blizzard.

"Yeah."

"Good. Get some on your face, too, and your hands and feet."

"I think I'm o—"

"You can't know if you are or aren't frostbitten, not yet. Just put them on. I'll rig the storm blanket." The hi-tech thermal layer zips to the walls, quite low down, further reducing the space the heater needs to keep warm but lowering head height to almost nothing.

When it's half zipped up, I scramble into the double-size sleeping bag, squeezing in on the other side of Harry, pull off my sweater so I'll share more heat with Harry, then zip the blanket up the rest of the way. If the heater dies, that thermal layer is supposed to save us. Supposedly.

"Got a dry hat and gloves?" I ask, as I grope around, wrapping two foot frostbite packs around my feet by feel.

"Yeah. And I put some on Harry."

"Good. Let's fold this top down and pad it with this extra scarf."

With the top of the sleeping bag tucked over and sealed, we're as warm as we possibly can be. Fresh air is more than a little scarce, but a slight headache by the time the storm goes over is better than freezing. Especially with Harry in this condition.

Clumsily, with the aid of my flashlight, I locate the correct frostbite packs for my face and hands, and get them stuck in place. Then I wrap my arms around

Harry, trying to give him as much heat from my body as possible. Darryl's arms cross mine as she tries to do the same thing from the other side of him.

The noise of the storm dies away so suddenly that it makes my breath catch a little, even though I were waiting for it. Strange, eerie silence falls over us. And then the noises begin. *Ping. Ting. Ping. Crack. Ping.* The metal in the 'Vi is contracting as the temperature plummets. Everything is contracting.

The eye is here.

"What do we do now?" whispers Darryl.

Only one thing left.

"Pray."

+

A familiar sensation of overheating wakes me. The eerie quiet has given way to gusting wind. Gentle gusts, compared to the howling blizzard that encircled the eye. It's over.

Quickly, I fold back the top of the sleeping bag. My reaching hands—made clumsy by frostbite-pack-gloves—touch the storm blanket, a bare foot above me, closing us in. I grope at the wall until I can unzip it and push that back too. Sitting up, I draw the sleeping bag away from Harry and Darryl and bend anxiously over Harry, checking…

He's breathing steadily. And when I press my forearm to his forehead…it's a normal temperature. Too hot, if anything, but that's what happens when you wrap yourself up this well and then the storm passes. Darryl is sound asleep too.

We made it. We survived the storm.

The frostbite packs on Harry's face have turned from black to clear, showing that their healing properties have discharged, just like the ones on my hands. I'd better get him some more.

He doesn't stir as I peel off the old ones, stick him new ones in place and double-check his temperature with an actual thermometer. Nor does Darryl. All that running and freezing last night… I'm not surprised.

I leave the sleeping bag folded down to their waists to reduce how much they overheat, and climb — *ouch, darn feet!* — down to the living area again, sliding the door shut to let them sleep on.

I sit for a moment while I wrap my abused feet in new packs, taking a moment to inspect them. Yeah, they're frostbitten. And cut. And bruised. But I reckon they'll heal. I ain't gonna lose no toes or nothing. That sure is a relief.

My happiness at our survival feels muted. Lethargic. My eyes go to the cab doorway, where the raptor slit Seb's belly clean open and began to eat him while he were still alive. The way they do.

Sorry, Seb. But you didn't even leave us with so much as a belt knife. And you can't calibrate a raptor. Once you point it at someone and pull the trigger — it's gonna do what it's gonna do.

I almost add, *I did tell you not to come out*, but then, I told him that precisely to make sure he would, so it don't really count. Heck, I wish Darryl hadn't been involved.

Feet treated, I limp to the console and wake it up, swiping quickly through folders as I check exactly what's missing.

Everything.

My family files—photos, messages, paperwork, etc.—ain't the problem. I've got out-vehicle backups, of course I have, including physical drives with Technicolor, just like I've got their backup drives hidden in the bottom of my gun cabinet.

But the camera footage…

I look in the video folders a second time, but they really are empty. Seb deleted the footage of him arriving at the 'Vi, deleted all the footage up until we escaped.

Quickly, I check the Net back-up log.

There *was* a satellite lock during those long hours we were driving and the footage *did* upload!

But…darn it! Seb deleted it after we escaped, when he got another satellite lock. And the footage since we got out of the 'Vi…never even existed. Seb switched off the recording function right away. An administrator can do that, though it ain't considered sensible—not if you've nothing to hide.

Seb taking over the 'Vi.

Holding us prisoner.

Us escaping.

Darryl and me climbing back in, battered and panicking.

Seb getting eaten…

There's no footage.

There's no proof of how none of it went down.

Thank God we cleaned up so well last night.

For a while I just sit, alternating between icy fear at our situation, and fury at Seb for putting us in this position. But sitting around ain't gonna help us, however much I wanna stay off my feet.

I'd better start cleaning.

First, I've absolutely gotta pee.

I open the extending bathroom door, step inside, flicking it automatically so it locks into position, enclosing part of the living area for extra space. I bend to fold down the toilet bowl, which will open the head's hatch to the incinerator—then pause.

A familiar ugly plastic gallon jar lies in the corner. *What the—?* How did *that* get in here?

Oh no…

Seb's cruel voice speaks in my memory: *He was little enough use alive, he's no use at all dead. You may as well just empty it down the head.*

Frozen by a desperate, desperate desire for it not to be true, it takes me a moment to make myself move, to pick up the urn, to turn it over…

The lid *is* off. It *is* empty. Nothing but a tiny sprinkling of ash on the floor. Which means…

I stare at that little hatch to the incinerator. I can't breathe. I almost feel like I do when I'm having a phobic attack, 'cept we're out-city. I drop to my knees and just barely retain the sense to slam my fist into the shaggy shower mat, folded neatly to one side, instead of the metal floor. I slam my fist into it over and over.

"Devil take you, Seb! Devil take you!"

Too late, right?

I clutch the empty jar to my chest, and flop back against the wall, gasping, gasping, and wanting to cry more than I've wanted to cry in a long time.

But the tears just won't come. I'm safe, right? I'm in the 'Vi, Seb is dead, and the storm is passed. I'm safe. Why can't I cry? Did going to prison break something in me?

"I'm sorry, Wilhelm," I whisper at last. "I'm so sorry." I've let him down so bad.

Eventually, the shaking and gasping tail off, and I make myself move again. It's a quick job to open the floor hatch and lift out the ash box. Carefully, painstakingly, I pour it all back into the jar, though I ain't quite sure if it's the right thing to do. At least the head's not been used much since I left jail. I'd better ask Father Ben, I guess. But right now, what else *can* I do? I guess God can deal even with this.

"Seb, you snake," I whisper. "I hope you *are* in

hell."

But where else would he be, after this, after... everything?

I have to shake the jar over and over to make the ash sift down as compactly as possible, but I squeeze every flake back into it. All of Wilhelm is in there, leastways. The extra stuff...I ain't thinking about that.

I take the jar back out into the living area and open the cupboard. No sign of the nice dino gift bag. Guess it's in the urn too, now. I open the gun cabinet instead and place the urn safely in the bottom. Sure, I'm switching the fence on after the herd's already gone through it, as Darryl would put it—but it'll make me feel better to have it locked up, after this.

My gaze rises to the top of the gun cabinet, to the little explosives box at the top. The place where, while Darryl, Harry, and I were on the run, the pyx from their farm nestled in our little home tabernacle. It's empty now, and the 'Vi don't feel the same without Him.

I kneel for a moment anyway, in honor of what used to be in there. And 'cause I desperately need a moment to calm myself. Seb's vicious, senseless act, hitting just when I thought we were safe, has shaken me up real bad.

But as the memory of our Divine passenger soothes my soul, guilt stirs. Heck, I am *so, so* angry with Seb right now. But he's dead. He's paid. Anything more he needs to pay, God will deal with that. And *we* cut short the time he mighta had to see the light—me and Darryl. Even if we didn't do nothing wrong, the weight of that fact presses onto me, all of a sudden.

"Yeah, I'm, uh…I'm sorry, Lord," I whisper. "I didn't mean what I said. If he snuck into purgatory somehow—I'm okay with that."

I still feel as though I could punch his teeth out, though—or sic another raptor on him.

I've *gotta* make myself forgive the snake fully. But how?

DARRYL

Sweat trickles down my face, my back, my neck. I am so hot.

I open my eyes. The familiar sight of the 'Vi's Master Bedroom ceiling meets my eyes. Familiar, and yet it feels like I haven't seen it much for some time. Something clings to my ears, my nose, my cheeks…my hands fly up, searching—but they're covered in thin squishy plastic glove-things…

Frostbite-packs?

Memory catches up in a rush. I turn my head, my breath pausing.

Harry lies beside me, breathing slow and deep. Fresh frostbite packs have been stuck to his nose and ears, and his hands too, no doubt.

For a few moments, I just watch him. I almost feel like I'm floating, I'm so relieved. He's okay. We made it back to him in time!

Then the heat drives me from the doubled-up double sleeping bag. Josh is already gone. How are his feet?

Harry doesn't stir as I shift to the end of the berth and climb down, so I slide the door closed to reduce the chances of waking him. He must be beyond exhausted.

How long did I sleep? I glance at the time. It's mid-afternoon, assuming I didn't sleep the clock around. The light level is low, the early winter evening combining with the trailing edge of the storm clouds to bring an early dusk.

Josh is in the living area, stuffing food into the OmniProcessor. When he glances at me, his face is paler than usual, his eyes strained.

"You think Harry's okay?" I ask him, feeling oddly awkward in his presence. We killed a man together, just hours ago...

He smiles tensely, hitting the start button. "Sure. I took his temperature when I renewed his packs, and it's back up to normal. We're gonna have to bring him to the emergency room to have his frostbite treated and his ankle set—but I don't think it's too bad."

A last knot of tension eases. Well, the last Harry-related knot of tension. My guts feel like they're stretched out on some ancient weaving loom. A loom made of spikes. "Good. That was way too close."

"Tell me about it." Josh sounds unusually grim.

"How are your feet? You shouldn't be walking on them."

"I reckon they're gonna be just fine. And not walking on them ain't gonna be an option for a while yet. We're still stuck up a mountain, y'know."

A slight tightness inside me relaxes, though, at his confident prediction. I reckon he's seen more frostbite than I have. "Can we eat something before we clean? I don't think I can wait for whatever you're cooking." When did we last eat? Yesterday morning, right? "And you'd better let me see to your feet. And your arm…"

"We've gotta do something else, first. Before Harry wakes up."

"What?"

Josh limps to the fridge, removing a scentBlock bag. "We gotta bury this, decent, like."

I peer at it. I can't see anything except what looks like scraps of torn shirt all bundled up with something.

"What is—?" I break off as I make out the dark stains on the fabric. Suddenly I'm glad I haven't eaten yet. "Is that…?"

"The few bits that were left in here, yeah."

"And you want to…? Wouldn't it be better to…put it down the head?" Reduce it safely to ash… As soon as the words have left my mouth, I feel bad. Human remains should be buried. That's what Father Ben would say.

"We did what we had to do, Darryl, but we *need* to bury this. Do it right. For us as well as for him. Sure, it'll be out here, and no one will ever know, but we can't do nothing about that. I've been monitoring for half an hour, so we can go straight out, get it done."

Josh climbs quickly up to the turret for a final check, while I set up a message to auto-send to Dad next time we have satellite lock to let him know we're okay. But, soon enough, we're crouched in the snow behind a boulder that screens us from the 'Vi—just in case Harry does wake up—while Josh digs through the snow and earth with a folding trowel.

"Okay, that'll do," he says before that long. Either he's still very tired, or he's just not that bothered if something eats the rest of Seb. Although, I guess the hole is deep enough to deter small scavengers and we're not burying enough to tempt large ones, even without the ScentBlock layer.

He places the bag in the bottom of the hole and stares down at it for a few moments, his expression shifting as though he's feeling super-mixed emotions.

"Well, Seb," he says at last in a tight voice, "you were a real unpleasant guy, but I wish it hadn't ended like this. I sure hope you lived long enough at the end there to make your peace with God. Probably too much to hope you even thought about it. But I guess we'll pray for you, just in case it'll do any good."

We would? I try not to grimace too obviously. This guy tried to kill my little brother, to kill Josh, and me... Dad, too.

Josh is looking at me, so I guess he thinks I should speak as well. I struggle to get a grip on my thoughts and emotions. Of course I have to forgive him. Just like I had to forgive Wilhelm. However little I want to.

"We'll, uh, pray," I manage. "Er...good luck."

Which is a stupid thing to say, but what do you say at the funeral of the man who tried to murder you? That is, at the clandestine burial of a few scraps of his flesh? When there seems to be a super-high chance that he's burning in hell?

Josh seems satisfied, anyway. We cross ourselves and quickly shove the earth back into the hole. Josh presses it down hard with the shovel and spreads snow over the top, and we hurry back to the 'Vi.

It's done.

And I guess it does actually make me feel a little better. That painful tension eases—just slightly.

HARRY

I'm so hot. Which is weird, because the last thing I remember is being colder than I can ever remember being. I'm still more tired than I ever remember being, though.

Eventually, after a million years, I drag my eyelids open and stare up at an unfamiliar ceiling. It's only when, a few thousand years later, I turn my head and look around some more, that I realize I'm in the 'Vi's Master Bedroom. Darryl's berth, as it used to be.

What happened? Why does thinking feel like slogging through deep, sticky mud?

Oh. It all swims back.

Seb. That endless night. Running. The mountain pass... My ankle... Waiting alone in the crack...

Something swells in my chest, something enormous and painful and wonderful.

They came back. They survived, and they came back in time. With the 'Vi!

I'm so tired, I don't want to do anything but lie here. But I'm so hot. And hungry. And I've really gotta pee. But pain stabs through my ankle when I move it. And my hands are engulfed in squidgy treatment packs, making it hard to even unzip the sleeping bag all the way.

Did they? The thought drops suddenly, sickeningly, into my mind. *Did they* both *survive?*

"Darryl? Josh?" I yell, my voice cracking in panic.

A moment later, both their faces appear in the little doorway.

"Harry?"

"Hey, you okay, little bro?"

I've barely finished bursting into tears when I'm

wrapped in a big double hug.

Thank you, Lord! Thank you!

DARRYL

It's far harder to get Harry down than it was to get him up there, but once Josh has fitted an ankle brace to his broken joint, we're able to lift him out with minimum wincing. At least from him. My muscles have never been this stiff in my life.

Josh and I ate some cold food earlier but, after deep cleaning for several hours, we're both ready for another meal—and a break.

It's the most wonderful feeling, just sitting at the table eating with Harry and Josh. I've never really thought of myself as taking them for granted—I know better than that, right?—but now...

I keep catching them shooting looks at me and each other, and I keep doing the same. Guess none of us can quite believe that we're all still here.

"So?" demands Harry, when he's eaten his last bite and drunk his last sip and stared at his plate in weary satisfaction for a few minutes.

"So, what?" inquires Josh blandly, sipping his own drink.

"So," says Harry, "how'd you get the 'Vi back? Where's Seb?"

We killed him, little bro. We killed him. It sounds so

odd in my head.

"Seb's a long way from here," says Josh. "And we don't never have to worry about him again, okay?"

"So he's dead?

"He won't be bothering us no more. That's all you need to know about it."

"Are you kidding me? Is the dirty raptor dead or alive?"

"It's all dealt with. We have the 'Vi back. Everything is fine."

Fine? Slowly, I wind my braid around my finger, barely aware I'm doing it. I'm not quite sure if I entirely believe that, when my guts still feel like they're being stretched out to the moon and back. For a moment Seb's shrieks echo in my head. I know he was literally storming out of that cab to kill us—or worse. And yet... I shake my head slightly, trying to get rid of the sounds.

"Ryl!" Harry protests, turning to me. "What happened?"

"You heard Josh." I force myself to speak calmly. "Everything's dealt with."

"Why won't you tell me?"

"Because we can't talk about this, Harry, do you understand? Seb deleted all the videos that showed what happened yesterday. So nobody can know that Seb brought us out here, not *anyone*, not *ever*."

He glares at me, but I stare him down harder than

I ever have in my life, as I add, "Not even Dad, Harry. Not even Dad."

JOSHUA

The snow piled up around the front and driver's side by the storm has frozen harder than hard. I have to take the pickaxe out and hack through it, foot by foot by foot, until the vehicle's free. Fortunately, it's only along one side, so it's fairly easy to get ourselves loose. Darryl insists on taking regular turns to rest my feet, but she ain't strong enough to make quick work of it.

Except for up against large objects like the 'Vi, the high wind has left most of the mountainside fairly snow-free. With the winter tracks on, once we're free, we only have to stop a couple of times to shovel a path through particularly enormous drifts—though that's hard enough, the way we're feeling.

We make it back down to the stopping place as full dark is falling, and it's with considerable relief that I switch off the engine. My feet are killing me. My arm, too.

Harry's been slumped in the front seat, where he insisted he was well enough to sit, his head lolling, snoring loudly for most of the hairy descent. But now he raises his head with a grunt. "Why are we stopping? We've got to get back to Dad!"

"It's dark, Harry. And I'm tired." Understatement. All that hacking and digging on top of last night was the final straw. "We have to stop for the night, okay?"

Harry grumbles, but Darryl frowns at him until he falls silent—then promptly yawns and nods off again.

HARRY

Darryl and Josh are so quiet as we drive, the next day. Just tired? Worried what's going to happen when we get in-city?

Yeah, I wish I believed that.

One of them killed Seb. They can refuse to tell me that all they like, but it's obvious. I mean, Seb has to be dead, right? Even if they just put him out of the 'Vi and left him, the storm woulda killed him, just the way he meant us to die when *he* drove off.

But I reckon one of them had to put a spear through him. Or something.

The guy had it coming in spades. But that probably doesn't make it any easier when you're the one who actually has to do it.

I guess I can see why they're so adamant we can't talk about what happened. Why they don't want me to know the details. They're scared. They don't know how to prove they didn't do anything wrong. The only way they won't ever have to prove it is if no one knows. Ever.

I wish they'd tell me. I want to know so badly. But I know they're trying to protect me as well as them.

But there shouldn't be any problem, right?

I mean, who's gonna miss a guy like Seb? He's already wanted for murder. So if the cops can't find him, they'll just think he's hiding from them. Josh and Darryl are worrying too much.

I've stopped asking them already, though. They've both got that look in their eye. The look that tells me I'm gonna have to get used to not knowing.

But I can't stop wondering.

Was it Josh?

Or was it…Darryl?

My big sis…

It's such a weird thought.

My gaze strays to Josh's booted foot as it presses the gas pedal up and down while he maneuvers over the newly-snowy landscape, up and down. Pain tightens his face. Hopefully we'll soon reach terrain where he can let Darryl drive. I finally saw what had happened to his feet this morning, when Darryl changed the dressings. Made me feel real bad about hassling him to travel overnight to get back to Dad sooner. I can't believe he's driving *now*. His feet must be in agony.

Just like the day we met, I guess.

DARRYL

Josh remains quiet as we drive.

We ain't done nothing wrong, that's what he said. It's what I *believe,* with my head.

So why does it feel so like we…like we *murdered* Seb?

'Cause we set him up, I guess. If he'd been pointing that gun straight at us, and *then* we threw a raptor at him…that would feel like self-defense. But we lured him out to his death, stone-cold deliberately — and to a darn horrible death, at that.

Stone-cold? For a moment, I'm hiding in the rear pen again, my heart pounding so hard I'm almost nauseous with nerves, head buzzing with terror that it's not gonna work, that Seb is about to storm back here and kill us both — or worse…

No, there was nothing cold about it.

But deliberate? Yeah, it was deliberate, all right.

We were desperate. And our only other choice was to let him kill us — to let Harry die — so I can't see how what we did *wasn't* self-defense, just like Josh says it was.

But…will it ever *feel* that way?

HARRY

Dad is almost purple with rage as he stares at poor Josh.

"How dare you. How *dare* you take my children out-city into that storm, how dare you let Harry—" Spluttering with rage, he simply waves a hand at me, top to bottom, as though he doesn't feel he *needs* to describe it in words.

I know I look like a mess. Thanks to Josh's top quality frostbite packs, I'm not gonna lose more than a superficial surface layer of flesh from my extremities, but my skin is horribly blackened all the same, nose, ears, fingers, and so on, far worse than Darryl's or Josh's, though we all look quite frost-grazed. And my ankle nestles in a brand new cast. It's not exactly hard to see why Dad's so mad. But...

Don't lie outright, I remind myself. *Just omit and imply.* That's what Josh and Darryl told me to do. It still feels wrong. Probably is. Especially to *Dad*. And yet...the Dad I remember—the thought of not telling him would be crazy. But this new, moody Dad? I just don't know how he'd react.

"Dad," I say as calmly as I possibly can, "It wasn't Josh's fault, okay? You were supposed to have police interviews all morning, right? We should have had plenty of time for a quick drive, but we got caught in the lightning-freeze. The *unforecasted* lightning-freeze. Obviously we had to sit it out, meaning we were out-city much longer than ideal, and we're really sorry that worried you. But it isn't Josh's fault."

"A drive? You've got a broken ankle! And *frostbite!*

You were *out-'Vi!* All of you!"

"That was my fault," I say quickly. "Not Josh's. I was stupid, okay? But Josh and Darryl took good care of me." I *did* do something stupid, very stupid, letting myself get so out of shape in-city.

"He took you both out there without my permission. And let you get hurt! He's the adult, so it *is* his fault..."

"Dad," there's a slight sharpness to Darryl's voice, "Josh doesn't need your permission to take me anywhere. I'm an adult too, remember? And I was the one who said Harry could come, not Josh."

"You're not Harry's next of kin! *I am.*"

"Sorry, Dad. I guess we just forgot." Darryl manages to speak in a soothing voice, but Dad scowls harder than ever.

"You just *forgot*? You don't have the *right* to give Harry permission to do things like that!"

"I said I was sorry, Dad." Darryl's really on edge now, though she's trying to keep her temper. "You haven't been around, okay? So don't give us a hard time about this. We didn't *mean* to get caught in that storm. We didn't *mean* to worry you."

"Didn't *mean* to worry me?" explodes Dad. He jabs his finger toward Josh, who stands still and quiet just inside the hospital room door, his own injuries far less visible than mine. "You were gone *two nights*! I've half a mind to file kidnapping charges!"

"Kidnapping charges?" I wince as Darryl's voice shifts from forced calm to full-out rage. Oh boy. *"Kidnapping charges?* Who are you going to file them against? *Me?"* She's almost screaming, but then her voice drops to an intense whisper. *"I looked out for Harry for two years while you were drinking beer in that snug little house Mau set up for you! Did you care about us then?* I can't *believe* you—"

Coldness washes over me as Dad jerks back as though she struck him. Heck, how did I not realize before how *angry* she is with Dad?

Did *she?*

But Dad's shock quickly swells into renewed anger. "How dare y—!"

Josh unfolds his arms and backs through the door. "I think it's best if I just go, Darryl," he says softly. "Let everyone calm down."

"Don't tell me to calm down!" shouts Dad. But Josh is gone.

Darryl draws herself up very straight, glaring at Dad. "It was *not* Josh's fault. Period. And he worked *so* hard to keep us safe and get us back here as quickly as possible once the storm was over! You should be *grateful!"*

With that, she turns and stalks out of the room after Josh.

As I stand there with Dad, who's still breathing hard after all the shouting, my stomach knots itself into an icy lump, almost as though I'm back in my crack in the storm.

"Dad," I say softly, desperate to make him understand. "It *wasn't* Josh's fault, okay? It was—it was mine."

Yeah, far, far better he blames me. I really, *really,* wish we could tell Dad everything, the way he's reacting—but Darryl made me *promise* I wouldn't, and I do get why. But Dad hadn't exactly taken a liking to Josh, even before.

But Josh is our family now too. What if Dad can't accept that?

I'm so scared he's going to try to drive Josh away. Because if he does that...

I stare at the doorway, through which Darryl has just disappeared.

Dad's just seen exactly what will happen.

A cold, wet piranha'saur seems to have got inside my stomach, nipping sharply at me.

Seb's gone. But is he going to destroy everything, anyway?

Don't miss Book 12 –
A Nest of Piranha'saurs

Coming Soon!

Don't miss the rest of
the unSPARKed series.

PICK UP BOOKS 1-10 TODAY!

DON'T FORGET THE PREQUELS!

DON'T MISS

A MOM WITH BLUE FEATHERS

An unSPARKed Prequel

Set 9 years before WEIGH THE ODDS.

When Joshua is separated from his family on the eve of his eleventh birthday his dad, Isaiah, and his Uncle Z know they may never see him again alive.

With the Habitat Vehicle out of action, Isaiah soon faces the most difficult decision of his life. Should he leave his brother Zechariah to work on the stranded vehicle alone while he sets off on foot in a desperate search for his son?

Meanwhile, alone in the dinosaur-infested wilderness, young Joshua is putting into practice all the survival skills his dad has taught him—until an unexpected encounter with a deadly predator sets the stage for the most unlikely alliance imaginable.

COMING SOON!

TURN OVER FOR A SNEAK PEEK

A MOM WITH BLUE FEATHERS

JOSHUA

Feet away, the fully-grown Dakotaraptor—as tall as Dad and many times longer—stands looking right at me. My heart pounds, *thud, thud, thud, thud,* each stroke so hard it hurts, and a strange ringing fills my ears as I stare at my death. I wanna run for the cliff, but the raptor will be on me in one bound. My body's shaking, and I'm furious with myself, 'cos only little kids move when there's a predator around.

The raptor raises her muzzle, sniffing...about to spring? For a moment I'm afraid I'm gonna wet myself, even though I'm eleven. Or just run away, screaming like an idiot.

But I can hear what Dad said to me, once. *Someday, Josh, there might come a time when it's over and there ain't nothing that will save you. Then there's only one choice left—whether to take it like a man.*

When Dad imagines this moment, that's what I want him to picture. Me taking it like a man.

And I want it to be true.

I'm not gonna run. I'm not gonna scrabble at the

cliff like a panicked puppy while she drags me down from behind.

I stand straight and look her in the eye—and wait.

DAY 1 - *29 hours earlier*

ISAIAH

"There are plenty of fish!"

Zech has only just given the all-clear, and it feels like my hand's barely withdrawn from the door control, but Josh is already down by the stream, peering into the rippling water.

"Look, Dad! Perch, trout...salmon, see!"

His ten-year-old voice is pitched low, despite his excitement, carrying back up the bank to me but not much further. His Uncle Z's on watch in the Habitat Vehicle's turret, of course, rifle in hand, but it's always better not to draw attention. We'd rather be outside enjoying the September sun and the fishing than sitting in the HabVi waiting for a prowling carni'saur to clear off.

"Well, don't catch them all before I get my turn." My big brother's voice comes over my earpiece, and Josh's. Josh and I have switched off the audio between our two, since we'll be outside together.

I glance around again, admiring the safety of the site. Behind us towers a high cliff, which extends along the right side of the open area, split only by a couple of ravines—one just large enough to drive through, as we proved yesterday evening when we arrived. On the left it's not really cliffs, but an extensive area of boulders and crags that make it a less than ideal approach for any large carni'saur.

On the far bank of the small river or mountain stream—it's poised between the two, size-wise—an area of grass and vegetation stretches away, but the river's just deep and fast enough to create a bit of a barrier, making this near-as-never-mind our own private beach. Zech—or me, when it's my turn—can set the movement sensors to cover the cliffs and boulders at the rear and sides, and concentrate mostly on that open land across from us. Sweet.

I drop from the HabVi's side door, leaving it open in case we need to make a quick retreat at some point, and head down the slope, carrying my fishing pole, gear, and a cooler with a few snacks and drinks.

"We'll never catch them *all!*" Josh tells Zech, still staring into the water. "There're so many this year."

"Guess they had a good summer." I find a comfortable spot to settle on the bank's rather dry grass, make sure the cooler's stable, and start laying out my fishing gear.

By the time I'm ready to cast, Josh has already kicked his boots off, waded out into the shallows, and taken up a position on a flat rock, his thin, sleek fishing spear held ready.

"Sure you don't wanna use a pole?" I tease him.

"It's so much more restful."

"And boring!" *Plop!* The spear flashes down into the stream and emerges with a flapping fish on the end. Josh gives the spear a sharp flick, with an extra little twist to free the fish from the barb. *Splat*—the fish lands on the bank nearby, splashing me.

"Hey!"

Josh snickers. "Sorry! Come on, slow poke, or I'll catch more than you!"

I roll my eyes. Even Zech, who's way more competitive than me, doesn't pretend to be able to out-fish my son. Josh is like a heron with that spear of his.

I cast, place the pole into its holder and settle back on the bank in the sun, watching Josh—*plop-splat*—fishing with an efficiency I can't hope to match. Still, no need to worry about catching enough to justify the trip. Zech and I can simply relax, and Josh will fill the fish-locker for us and enjoy every minute of it.

Plop-splat.

I take a bottle of juice from the cooler. It's the last of our city-bought apples. But the wild apples will be ready to gather soon. Josh is pretty handy at that, too. Climbs like a monkey. Sometimes Zech says he wonders how we ever managed without him.

Plop-splat.

He's eleven tomorrow. How is that even possible? Seems no time since I were carrying him around in a sling on my front, gurgling happily. Or that he were crawling around my feet on days like this, chirping back to any bird or 'saur nearby.

Eleven. He's still a child—just. He's already so sensible and level-headed. Only a few more years, now, and he'll be a man, pretty-much.

And he'll be a good one. Such a kind nature and a strong sense of right and wrong. Still, it's so hard to imagine. My little Joshua...

Despite the approaching fall, it's warm in the sun today, as the long, hot summer still refuses to yield its grip. I could happily take a nap, but Zech or no Zech, I'm not doing that while Josh is out-vehicle with me. I sip more juice. I don't have to stay on high alert, but I do have to stay awake...

Plop-splat.

A huge trout cascades me in water as it splashes down on the bank.

"Aw, come on, Josh!"

"You looked like you were nodding off!"

"Were not. That's one fine fish, though. That will do for dinner."

"Don't I get to pick?" says Josh. "If Christmas and Easter start at nightfall then by dinner-time Saint Des would say it's my birthday, right?"

Zech snorts from my earpiece.

I shrug. "Well, I guess you could argue it that way, little lawyer. Your birthday being a special occasion and all. Yeah, you can pick."

"Okay. But not until it's time to cook. I might catch a better one by then!"

"You might, at that. You are unbelievable with that spear of yours."

JOSHUA

I shrug Dad's praise away and turn back to the teeming water. Why do he and Uncle Z make such a big thing about my spear-fishing? Anyone could do it, right? You just watch, and you can guess which way they're gonna go and then...

Plop.

I flick the fish onto the bank—*splat*—a little further from Dad, this time. It's funny when they splash him, but if he gets too soggy he'll wanna go back into the 'Vi. Even with the strong sun, there's a slight nip of fall in the air, biting at my bare feet. Some years it rains on my birthday, but tomorrow...I glance at the sky. Yeah, unless something changes a lot by this evening, tomorrow we'll still have sun! We can fish and chill out all day.

*Umm, look at that one...*I track a plump trout until...*yes...*

Plop. Got'ya. I flick it to shore. *Splat.*

"I still think we shoulda tried the ice rink again," says Uncle Z in my ear, obviously talking to Dad.

I shoot a glare at the turret, then turn back to the water and try to ignore them.

"He don't wanna go to a city-rink." Dad's voice gets a slight edge to it, like it always does when they're arguing about how best to deal with my...problem. "He don't wanna go in-city, period."

"Yeah, but he's gotta, hasn't he? Sometimes. Why not practice getting him to leave the 'Vi for something fun?"

"Because it ain't fun for him!" snaps Dad. "I'm not torturing him for his birthday treat!"

"He's gotta learn to cope with—"

"I've already said he's going with me or you to the store and the shop *every* time we go in-city from now on, haven't I? He's old enough now people won't look twice, even if we are clearly hunters. Now give it a rest and keep your eyes open. It's his birthday, for Pete's sake. Almost."

Uncle Z shuts up at last and I stare into the water, trying to concentrate. But I miss my next thrust.

What did Uncle Z have to bring that up for? I hate cities so much.

It didn't used to matter. Dad and Uncle Z never used to even *let* me leave the 'Vi—not that I wanted to. Only after dark. Then I were allowed to venture out with them and join the other hunters around the firepit or grill or whatever the 'Vi-park had for a gathering place. Never in daylight.

I didn't rightly understand why, 'til they took five-year-old me to that Father Morris to arrange a baptism—they thought I were old enough by then that he wouldn't freak out when he realized I live in the HabVi all the time. But, boy, did he. The priest and Dad ended up having a tug of war over me right there in the church parking lot—I were crying, all the adults were shouting—sick shudders still run through my belly at the memory.

Dad and Uncle Z ran away—literally ran—carrying me, leaving that Father Morris screaming after them that he were gonna call...someone or other, and they would...something or other, but it boiled down to taking me away from Dad and locking me up in-city.

We left behind a load of rubber on the pavement of the 'Vi-park and a ton of expensive gear that were being serviced in the shop, and crossed the border into Yoming State only a few hours later. Didn't come back to Exception State until I were seven, though we liked it better here. By then Dad and Uncle Z weren't so worried. I could go outside in the 'Vi-park, any time. Lots of hunters start taking their kids on short hunting trips from about seven onwards. But we've never been back to *that* city. And even *now* we don't go nowhere where someone might figure out that I live in the 'Vi full-time.

It were when I were seven that I saw that amazing video of people ice-skating—just flying over the ice—and Dad and Uncle Z took me to a rink for my birthday. First time I left a 'Vi-park—almost all of which are right on the outskirts of the city, just inside the fence—since I were five, which were the last time we dared go to church—and we always went to the closest one of those, Christmas and Easter only.

I'd never wanted to go further into no city, but when I did, to go to the rink, I found I actually couldn't stand it *at all*. Felt like the roof were gonna fall on me. Like the place were about to chew me up and eat me. Like I couldn't breathe, trapped there among all those buildings and people and artificial scents and sounds.

I guess it were only then that Dad and Uncle Z realized there were something wrong with me. They've been arguing about how to fix it ever since. Uncle Z favors a tougher approach; thinks I should learn to grin and bear it. Dad's more understanding.

It's so not what I wanna think about on my almost-birthday. Thanks for nothing, Uncle Z!

Plop. I miss another thrust.

"Come have some juice, Josh," calls Dad. "You've already been at it a while."

Yeah, there's quite a heap of fish. I should gut them and get them into the freeze-drier.

I splash to shore and put my spear beside Dad's useless fishing pole, resting there in its mount. He offers me the juice, but I shake my head.

"I'm gonna sort these out first."

He smiles. "Ah, you're Mr. Responsible, you are. You're right, though. Let's get them done."

Josh squats on the bank on the other side of the heap of fish, pulls out his belt knife and sets to work, guts into a biodegradable starch bag I've taken from my gear, clean fish into a second. I draw my own hunting knife and do the same. I know Zech's upset him, bringing up his city-phobia in his usual insensitive way, and I were hoping we could have a little chat and something from the cooler and take his mind off it—but he's right. We don't want a carni'saur to show up, following the gathering scent of fish blood, nor do we want his fine catch to spoil in the sun.

"These are excellent fish."

"Yeah." He doesn't look up from his work, his knife flashing swiftly over a silvery perch.

I think a swearword at my big brother, up there in the turret. He doesn't seem to get that this ain't just some little dislike Josh has. I can't watch my son going white and clammy and gasping for breath and think that he just needs to *try harder*. No. He needs very small doses; build up gradually.

I mean, it's not like he's ever gonna wanna live in-city. His idea of a birthday treat is to go to the wildest region Zech's prepared to burn the fuel driving to and spend as much time out-'Vi as possible, fishing and enjoying nature. He's just gotta be able to bear the city for a few days at a time, enough to leave the 'Vi to do what servicing and store replenishment is necessary while he's there.

Zech's just worried, I guess. I mean, I am, too. We weren't so concerned when we first realized that Josh's uncomplaining compliance with staying in the 'Vi all those years stemmed from something rather more serious than mere obedience to us. We figured a bit of practice and he'd get over it. But it's been three years and his progress is so slow. But why did Zech have to bring it up *today*?

I toss the final fillet into the clean fish bag. "There. Well, that's a good start." We try to combine a birthday trip for Josh with filling our fish-locker. These mountains are bursting with streams—and the streams with fish. "Good job, Josh."

Josh smiles, and before I can think about getting up, he's grabbed one bag in each hand and bounded up the riverbank to the 'Vi. It looms 'bout sixty feet away, towering above us with its steel window shutters, huge wheels, and massive ground clearance, the full observation turret sticking up from the middle of the roof. The light armor glints in the sun. Well, light, compared to a tank. The cliff and the mountain range rising into view behind dwarf our happy home, even so.

Josh hasn't had much of a growth spurt yet and the floor is still above his head, but he springs up at the doorway without pausing, one foot landing precisely in one foothold, the other in the second, and with a vaulting leap, he's inside, his hands never touching down. I don't bother to call, "Don't forget to shut the freeze-dryer." That sort of comment just ain't necessary no more.

I hear the clang of the freeze-dryer's door closing, then the low roar of the incinerator as he drops the bag of fish guts to its fiery fate. And then he's leaping down from the doorway and racing to join me again, arriving beside me in a puff of sandy dust.

"Want some juice now?"

"Yeah!"

I hand him the bottle and he drinks thirstily. "Thanks, Dad! Caught anything yet?"

"Nah. Not with you stirring the water up all the time."

"You're not even trying, admit it," says Zech.

I ignore him. So does Josh, drinking more juice.

"What, so now I'm getting the silent treatment?"

Josh looks round at the turret and makes a rude gesture, though not so rude I'd have to punish him for it. Yeah, Zech's really upset him.

"It's just 'cause he cares, y'know," I say softly.

"Well, mebbe he could *not care* until my birthday's over. That'd be good. Can we stop talking about it?"

"Oh, Josh, your Uncle Z and I won't always be here forever, y'know. One day you'll *have* to be able to do stuff in-city by yourself—"

"*Dad? Seriously?*" Josh's wail cuts me off.

"Ah, sorry, Josh. I won't mention it again. Hey, come 'ere." I put an arm around him and draw him in for a hug. He lets me, but without the enthusiasm he'd once have shown. It's the same now when we have a carni'saur or dangerous herbi'saur in the rear pen and I have him sleep in with me in the "master bedroom" for extra safety. He complies, 'cause we raised him obedient, wouldn't be safe no other way. But he don't do it excited at the novelty, no more, just grudgingly, obviously feeling it a slight to his approaching manhood. Heck, he's growing up so fast.

But he accepts the hug, and after a moment even leans into it for a while. Then he's on his feet, grabbing his spear and heading back to his fishing rock.

Plop-slat.

Another pile of fish begins to mount up, but the sun gets stronger and stronger. Josh and I are sweating as we gut them. When Josh comes bounding back after taking them to the 'Vi he gleefully strips off his shorts and T-shirt and starts rolling down the bank into the river—splash—over and over, with much giggling and laughter and satisfaction at the wet procedure.

I'm not hot enough to accept an invitation to join in, and simply enjoy watching him. No, he's not quite grown-up yet. We've got a year or two more.

Look out for A MOM WITH BLUE FEATHERS.
Coming soon!

ABOUT THE AUTHOR

Corinna Turner has been writing since she was fourteen and likes strong protagonists with plenty of integrity. Although she spends as much time as possible writing, she cannot keep up with the flow of ideas, for which she offers thanks—and occasional grumbles!—to the Holy Spirit. She is the author of over thirty books, including the Carnegie Medal Nominated I Am Margaret series, and her work has been translated into four languages. She was awarded the St. Katherine Drexel award in 2022.

She is a Lay Dominican with an MA in English from Oxford University and lives in the UK. She used to have a Giant African Land Snail, Peter, with a 6½" long shell, but now makes do with a cactus and a campervan.

Get in touch with Corinna...

Facebook: Corinna Turner

Twitter: @CorinnaTAuthor

Don't forget to sign up for

NEWS

&

FREE SHORT STORIES

at:

www.UnSeenBooks.com

All Free/Exclusive content subject to availability.